Willa's
NEW WORLD

Willa's NEW WORLD

Barbara Demers

Edited by Barbara Sapergia.
Cover painting by Dawn Pearcey.
Interior illustrations by Debra Demers-Bryan.
Cover design by Duncan Campbell.
Book Design by Karen Steadman.
Printed and bound in Canada.

The publisher gratefully acknowledges the financial assistance of the Saskatchewan Arts Board, the Canada Council for the Arts, the Department of Canadian Heritage, and the City of Regina Arts Commission, for its publishing program.

Canadian Cataloguing in Publication Data

Barbara Demers, 1959-
Willa's new world
ISBN 1-55050-150-X

1. Title.

PS8557.E467W54 1999 JC813'.54 C99-920147-6
PZ7.D39212Wi 1999

COTEAU BOOKS
401-2206 Dewdney Ave.
Regina, Saskatchewan
Canada S4R 1H3

AVAILABLE IN THE US FROM
General Distribution Services
4500 Witmer Industrial Estates
Niagara Falls, NY 14305-1386

For Steven, Tessia, Lief, and Colton

Table of Contents

LONDON, MAY, 1795

"You want to send her *where?*" The sea merchant's clothes were dark with whale oil and tar. His hair was stiff with salt and his breath stank, but he was first mate, my great-uncle had said, and I was to sail on this ship. "A young lass like her? By herself?" he continued.

"I'll pay you well, of course, and there is money for extras," my great-uncle said.

The sea merchant fished loose tobacco from a bright red trouser pocket and slowly filled a battered pipe before he replied. "It'll cost you," he said finally. "And if word of this reaches the London Governors, then it's on your head. We'll know nothing of her or how she came to be smuggled aboard. As for her, she's not to trouble us. We're Company men, not nursemaids."

I watched the sailors load huge kegs of liquor bound for York Factory on Hudson's Bay and tried to ignore my great-uncle's expostulations as they slowly reached agreement. Then he took me to one side. "The trip to Hudson's Bay is not an easy one, Willa," he said. "But I can't keep you here in London. With the pestilence raging you'd soon catch your own death."

I nodded. I had also heard the shocked whispers from the servants that as a now penniless ward – and a girl of fifteen years – I was unwanted by him.

"I made my fortune in the colony, you know," my great-uncle continued. "And working there builds character. Your brother would have done well. Why the plague takes the best of us and leaves…ah, well. That's the way of it. You'll leave on the morrow."

I curtseyed, though I could feel black fear rising and filling my throat. How was I to live? What was I to do once I reached Hudson's Bay? My great-uncle believed children were to be neither seen nor heard, and in my panic I feared he would abandon me right then if I opened my mouth.

"I'll show you where you're to stay," he said,

stepping forward and brushing past the sea merchant without a glance. Now that the deal was made, my great-uncle could afford to ignore him. As we stepped around crates and ducked packets thrown by busy workers, he led me down into a dark and malodorous hold.

"The animals will be loaded last," my great-uncle said, "since they hate to ride on water." He barked a laugh as he looked around. "Your meals will be light, lass, but there's no point in wasting good food since ye'll not keep it down. But that's the way it is." He turned away and started up the steep set of steps. As I started to follow he turned back. His face was in shadow. "You might as well stay here," he said. "There's nowhere else for you to go. Goodbye."

With those words he continued up the steps. I did not see him again.

)) ◗●◖ ((

The next morning we crossed the channel in rough seas and headed north to the islands of the Orkney. I knew the route one took to reach Hudson's Bay from my brother's tales; it had been his dream to travel there. I knew, therefore, that we sailed to the town of Stromness, Orkney, to pick up more supplies and workers, if satisfactory ones had been found, and the hardy Orkney cattle.

Shortly after we set sail, a sailor came below and set a cloth sack down on the dirty pallet where I had lain the night before. He said, almost gently, "From your great-uncle, miss." He handed me a chamber pot filled with hard biscuits and a flagon containing some liquid inside. "There's more above deck – ye'll need to get them yourself," he said. I took them, though I did not expect to partake of more. That changed as the days passed. Then I was merely grateful that the biscuits did not have weevils nor was the water yet stale.

Task accomplished, the sailor promptly left me alone again. I opened the sack and pulled out my one remaining dress. The others had been burned, I knew. My great-uncle had sent other items, including a much-worn coat – a servant's castoff, perhaps? The outer, leathern side of the coat was dark with grease and oil. The inside was a very soft brown pelt. I had become accustomed to grime, however, and without hesitation I tried it on. Though long and big, once I rolled up a furry cuff I thought it would serve. Its thick pelt would keep the rats from biting me while I slept and perhaps delay my death by freezing when the ship docked. I knew many men – explorers, scientists, fur traders, and others – had frozen to death in the area. As a manner of dying, it might be the least painful, I thought. Still, I could not bring myself to care about living, for now there was no one left alive dear to me, nor anyone to whom I was dear. My great-uncle had not troubled to hide his satisfaction in ridding himself of me.

I pulled the coat more closely around me. It had no buttons or other closure – it must tie with a sash, I thought. I looked back inside the bag. There was a small leather waist pouch and a thick, leather-bound book containing blank pages – a journal for me to keep, I realized, recalling the annual packet of letters and journals my great-uncle had sent my family via supply ship each year. My brother, Charles, had read them numerous times and corresponded regularly with my great-uncle – finding even the most trivial detail absorbing. I put the journal in the pouch, which I then tied around my waist beneath the warm coat. By enclosing this journal for my travails did my great-uncle expect me to live? Or were these things he had intended to leave to my brother? I did not know. The coat and the journal were a comfort nevertheless.

As our journey continued northwards, the waves got wilder and the rocking of the ship fiercer. Storms beset us. The ship began to creak in the howling winds and rain. I huddled in the hold, clinging to my pallet with one arm and covering my ears with the other in a vain attempt to muffle the noise. The seasickness that Charles had dreaded did not strike me. I thought he would have been pleased to know that. Still, there was misery and woe to endure in its place. The groaning of the ship's wooden sides reminded me of the Orcadian legends of old. I could almost see the Orcs – ferocious sea monsters whose iron teeth could tear a ship asunder. With each shriek of wind and grinding of wood, I thought one had burst through the ship in triumph. I thought often of my mother and Charles. Soon I too would be dead and with my family again.

After unmeasured time, I began to hear shouts and curses from the sailors above the sounds of the wind and the rain. I sat up, finally, for then I believed the worst was over. Soon we had anchored and I went above.

Stromness seemed a bleak and desolate place, flat as far as the eye could see, with only rock and scrub for relief. The violent winds continued to blow. I watched a meagre and motley crow gather to see the ship loaded. Some of these idlers were skinny lads, possibly from some poor-children's home, who stood and shivered in the wind – their too-small rags and listless misery reminded me of waifs in London. The sailors shook their heads in disgust. "Not a one who would survive the journey to York," they agreed amongst themselves. The sailors ate, drank, and made merry while straining to shove and squash every crate and creature in as tight as could be. I tried to stay out of their way.

Too soon we set out on open seas. It was a wretched time. Many weeks passed. I shared my dark space with panic-stricken cows and hens, even one pig for a short time. I was surrounded by crates and whiskey barrels. Not long after, I became ill, though I did not die.

Near the end of this wretchedness, the ship seemed becalmed, for once. I ventured up from the hold with my bucket of slops to toss over. The sea was as calm as glass. The sky was filled with large clouds that masked the sun. The sails had been lowered. To one side of the ship was an icy spike of a ghostly greenish white. Though too far away to touch, stark coldness emanated from it in almost physical waves. I looked at the thing in wonderment. After timeless moments, I slowly became aware of shouting coming from above. A small, wizened sailor had hoisted himself high up the rigging where he shouted directions to the sailors below.

A sailor passed me and I followed him to the side of the ship where he unhooked a long wooden stave. "Might we strike a berg?" I asked him.

He made a face and wagged a finger at me. "Don't even think it, lass! Salty will steer us clear. He'll watch up there for the deep ones that can crack a ship in two. We just let him and the steersman do their work, and make ready to shove the ship away from the wicked ones."

He swung the stave overboard and jabbed it at the berg, which was not close enough to the ship to be reached. He paused a moment to stare at it. Its insides had melted from the sun, but two icy spires still gleamed upwards towards the sky. As we watched, the sun emerged from behind a cloud and shone down on the frozen whiteness. I could see reflected in the centre of the iceberg a ruby glow; and then a whisper of rainbow colours swept across its ivory sides. Its beauty affected me as nothing else had for too long. For a moment I was glad that I had lived to see this cold jewel. How I wished my brother could have seen it also. Silently it sailed past us. Then I heard the wizened sailor shout from high above, and the sailor near me hauled in his stave and hastened away. I picked up my slop pot and returned to my place, to darkness, dirt, and misery. We reached the Hudson's Bay's rocky shores many days after.

FLYING MOON: AUGUST, WHEN THE YOUNG BIRDS FLY

We reached a place called Five Fathom Hole in mid-August, 1795. Someone had said there was no harbour at York Factory, and so we were now some miles from it. I carried my larger bag in my left hand and tried to hold my furry coat closed with my right. As the men hauled me out of the dark hold, my eyes watered from the unaccustomed light. I stumbled and dropped the bag from my great-uncle, which rolled back down the steep steps.

"Leave the bag, lass, and step into the York boat," one of the sailors said impatiently. "We'll be unloading the cargo soon enough."

In a few moments, I was making my way down

a wharf that extended a good distance from shore. I headed towards a jumble of rocks. A crowd of men talked with the sailors who had disembarked previously. Some boats had already begun the trip to York Factory, but apparently I was to wait awhile longer. When I perched on a rock to let my eyes clear and my stomach settle, swarms of small biting insects surrounded me, and I covered my nose and mouth to keep from breathing them in.

"Where's your guardians?" asked a hoarse voice from behind me. Feeling dizzy, I turned carefully. I still felt the rocking ship beneath me. I tried to think how to answer.

"Got guardians?" the man asked, coming close to me and putting his hand on my shoulder. He was short and shabbily dressed. His heavily lined face and hands were black with dirt. The familiar smell of vomit and sour breath washed over me, but he was not a sailor from my ship. I had gotten to know every face, every voice during the interminable voyage. The insects swarmed momentarily over to him and I removed my hand from my face.

"I'm waiting for them," I said, not untruthfully, since I was going to need somewhere to work and to live for a time. The man slackened his grip on my shoulder and looked around suspiciously. I breathed in carefully. The smell of whale oil, fish, and salt water was bracing.

"Come with me – I'll find them," he said. He didn't look like the helpful sort, especially when he grabbed my arm and wrenched me up. "You listen to me. No gabbing. Where's your bag? Got any valuables?" He dragged me along beside him, hurrying over to where certain items were being tossed heedlessly off the small boat onto the wharf. Some bags almost landed in the water. Other sailors gathered them up, hauled them down the wharf, and set them, none too gently, on the wet, rubbly ground. The more important cargo, however, was being unloaded carefully from the large ship into smaller boats, which immediately set off down the river.

I pulled away from the man and rubbed my arm while I looked uncertainly at the heap of goods. "It's a small sack," I said, "blue, with rope handles. I don't believe it has been unloaded as yet."

The man grabbed me again, and pushed me towards the pile. Some of the bags were already wet from the water. "That one." He pointed at a particularly large bag that, at one time, may have been blue. A faded Company emblem was faintly visible. "Take that one."

I shook my head. It was not mine.

He put his face close to mine and commanded, "Take it." Reluctantly, I walked to the water's edge and grasped the handles of the bag. By half lifting, half dragging, I able to haul it over to him.

"You're a useless bit," he sneered and grasped the handles of the bag. Looking left and right, but seeing no one paying us any attention, he grabbed my arm in one hand and picked up the bag in the other.

As he led me away from the shore, the man hissed at me to walk faster. As we got closer to one cluster of men, I saw some sort of official referring to a packet of papers and directing others. I remembered being told by the sea merchant who had taken my great-uncle's passage money that I needn't report on arrival. Many of the sailors, however, seemed to be receiving instructions on something.

"Am I to be registered first?" I asked the man.

He grunted, and spat near my feet. "None but sailors on this supply ship. No need to waste time with that. You'll be dead soon enough. Now shut your gob."

Though I well expected to die soon, I felt my stomach lurch uneasily. Some ways of dying are worse than others. I had survived plague and an ocean crossing, but my ending at this man's hands could be unpleasant. My eyes still burned from the sun's rays, hazy though they were, and I had a hard time keeping pace with him. After the ceaseless heaving of the ship, I could not manage the stillness of the land. I stumbled frequently as a result. The man's hand tightened on my arm, so that it was soon numb. I realized that I must escape from him, but how? In London I would have been able to run away, but here – where could I run to? Who would help me? By now we were too far from the group to call for aid. I almost lost hope, for I was unused to thinking for myself.

"Are you hiring me to work?" I asked. He pushed me towards a wooden cart attached to a hard-used ox. The animal looked closer to death than the ones that had come aboard ship at Stromness in the Orkney Isles.

"To work, yes. Hire, no. You'll soon find out that you work, or you die." He smirked and then said, "Well, you'll die anyway. But you might as well work until then."

I climbed awkwardly up to the seat behind the ox, only to be tipped into the back by the man as he climbed up as well. "No sitting with your betters," he growled. I landed hard on my elbow and barely rolled out of the way before the blue bag landed where I had been moments before. With a jerk, the cart began to move. The wooden wheels felt more octagonally-shaped than round. I could see through the boards of the cart to the rutted tracks below, but the biting air made the tears start. My troubles at home and now here began to close in on me. Was it possible my life could be made worse? I needed work, I knew. But working for this man would bring me trouble. But what could I do? I had no plan, nor experience in making one. I knew no one. I had no one. Determined to avoid that train of thought, I focused on an immediate problem. I was cold.

While the cart jolted along the ruts, I crawled over to the blue sack and wrapped my arms around it in an effort to get warm. One thing about the ship, crowded and awful though it was, I had not been cold. The edges of my skirt and around the coat sleeves that had gotten wet when I fished the sack from the water were already rimed stiff. I gulped down air and tried to look at my surroundings in an effort to get my bearings. Suddenly I heard the lash sing through the air and I winced for the ox. But the lash was for me.

"Stay away from that sack! You're not to steal from it!"

I crawled away to the edge of the cart, although I could feel a thin line of heat on my back and a razor-sharp cut where the end of the whip caught my hand. So he had heard me say the sack was not mine. My family's property had long been sold. I had nothing left of value to me by then anyway, except for my mother's locket, which I now wore safely hidden round my neck. It was engraved silver, and my mother had kept two miniatures inside: one of me and one of Charles, done just fifteen months earlier – a lifetime ago, considering all that had happened since then. Charles and I had insisted she be painted as well and, laughing, my mother had agreed. After her death, I placed this miniature of my mother in the locket in front of mine. Feeling the silver warm against my chest had helped quell my fears in London. Here it seemed cold comfort.

I looked at the willows and scrubby brush that grew on either side of the track. The sky, grey and drab and chill, reflected a land of few colours. The land was relatively flat and smelled of marsh. I could see trees, but they looked a long ways off. If I jumped off the cart, there would be nowhere to hide. I knew we weren't near York Factory, but I did not know how far away it was nor whether the track would lead me there.

The cart came to an abrupt halt. "Out!" the man ordered, and I stiffly climbed down. I followed as the man led the ox off the track and down a slope. After walking for some time, he stopped. He whistled repetitive notes and soon, seemingly from nowhere, a man emerged from the side of a small hill.

"Is this wretch the best you could do, Digger?" The man looked coldly at me and rubbed his chin. I saw a heavy gold ring with a large red stone glint on one hand. The red glow recalled the terrible beauty of the iceberg. Perhaps getting too near the man, as with the iceberg, would prove deadly. "They get positively worse every year. A girl, yet." He was dressed all in black. Beneath a heavy woolen knee-length coat, I could see a tailored shirt in a style that had been popular in London a few years before. Unlike the man called Digger, whose face was stubbled and dirty, this one was washed and shaven.

"Sailors said the pickings were bad, Master Dyer. They didn't pick up any lads," Digger said.

I wasn't surprised at his words. While my brother had said workers from the Orkney Isles were encouraged to become employees for the Company, the boys I had seen at Stromness had looked ill, and indifferent at the prospect of leaving their homes. Nor had the sailors seemed interested in bringing any boys aboard. Still, after leaving the Orkney Isles, I had been crammed in so tight it had been hard to breathe. The provisions and trade goods were given better care and attention than I; the goods were accorded more space too.

Digger continued, "The way those sailors were complaining you'd think they had it tough or something. Nothing like when I came over –"

The other man waved an arm at me, interrupting Digger. "Well, don't just stand there gawking. To work!"

I looked around me and hesitantly stepped forward. I had no idea what I was to do. I looked at Digger and he shoved me hard.

"You deaf as well as stupid? In there!" I looked past the other man and now could clearly see a roughly hewn, low opening in the hill. I hurried in.

A small fire burned at the entrance. A rabbit lay partially cut up on its own skin. I picked up the knife beside it and finished the job. Since a kettle filled with a liquid simmered over the fire, I dropped the pieces in. I looked around the earthen cavity. A well-travelled packsack slumped near one roughly dug and crumbling wall and I could see some duffel and blanketing inside an opened crate, but nothing else was visible. It didn't look lived in. Perhaps it was simply a meeting place. I heard lowered voices, and so I crept to the entrance and looked out. Digger had been pulling metal goods out of the big bag from the cart while the other man, Dyer, watched. A flour sack lay beside the larger blue bag and Digger began transferring some pots into it. As I watched, Dyer reached into the blue bag again and lifted up something gold that glistened and sparkled in the weak sun. He whistled softly, then brought the object to his lips. I must have moved, because he spotted me then.

"Leave off your spying." Dyer tucked the glittering object inside his woolen coat.

"Or you'll find yourself dead sooner than later," said Digger, who had finished with the pots and was rummaging through the bag again.

Dyer turned to me and said, "Get the kettle."

I hurried to do so, using my skirt to lift the kettle off the fire. There seemed to be no spoons or bowls, so I carried the kettle alone out to him. My stomach was contracting painfully. Meat had become too dear for us many months previously and now I no longer missed it. But to have something other than hard biscuit....

Digger reached over and grabbed the kettle from me so quickly that some of the liquid splashed onto my hand. I gasped in pain. He pushed me away. "Clumsy oaf!"

"Get away," Dyer said, and he gestured impatiently at me. I wrapped my hand in my skirt and went back to the hill's opening.

I watched the sky darken as night fell. The fire died down and then went out. I wrapped my great-uncle's coat more closely around me and huddled down against the side of the hill, where I must have fallen asleep. It was much colder though still dark when Digger shook me roughly. "Get up – we're going." Dyer had removed his pack from the hillside and was transferring goods from it to the flour sack.

Eventually Digger hefted the flour sack and Dyer's pack into the cart. He prodded the ox back up the trail to the track. I followed silently, terrified that Dyer would creep up on me unawares. I did not know why he had this menacing effect on me. He was not large, nor were his manners or bearing particularly unsavory. Digger's, in fact, were far worse. Dyer had no apparent odd or unusual features. But I greatly feared him.

When we got back on the cart's track, Digger motioned to me to get back in the cart. He pointed to Dyer's pack. "Sit on that. Spread your skirt over it." I obliged, and soon the cart was bumping along the narrow track. Dyer caught up with us and in one smooth motion swung himself up beside Digger on the seat. I held onto the side of the cart to keep from being bounced out. The ground was churned up in places from past rains and had dried in little clumps. Stones and dirt lumps cracked and broke under the squeaking wheels of the cart.

We passed the ship at Five Fathom Hole that was still being unloaded, slowly and carefully now, by a large group of early risers, into broad, shallow boats. Digger halted the cart. I saw no familiar faces nor my own bag. The men loading the boats must be Company men from York Factory, I surmised. Could the sailors from my ship have already transported themselves and their belongings to the Factory by boat? Would I have been in one of those boats if Digger hadn't waylaid me? The whole area surrounding the ship looked desolate. I looked down at my hands and realized, without really caring, that they were cold. I tucked them into the greasy coat sleeves and tightened my hold on the cart through the leathern fabric. Dyer, meanwhile, jumped down from the cart and sauntered over to where a boat was almost ready to leave the wharf. I heard shouts of surprise at the sight of him. After a moment's conversation the boatmen lifted a large crate back onto the wharf and Dyer climbed into the boat instead. I took a deep breath and felt the sick feeling in my throat subside somewhat. The man was gone from us. With a grunt, Digger switched the ox and we moved on.

Some hours later I smelled smoke. Soon after I heard sounds of human activity. As the cart bumped over a rise, I roused myself from the daze into which I had fallen and looked ahead past Digger. The land seemed to come to life in a swirl of colour and activity. Conical structures, which I had seen only in pencil sketches in my great-uncle's letters, magically rose up – large triangles with red and green and black designs painted on the outside. Others were lower, mounded structures covered in skins, bark, or some other material. After dreary months at sea and then bleak colours of sky and ground, the sheer variety of patterns, colours, and activity was startling. There were children running around the camp. Dogs ran after them, barking. Fires burned inside stone circles, and thin tendrils of smoke rose from inside the lodges. Women were tending to food and children, airing blankets and clothing, pounding dried things with stones, talking in small groups. Shouts and laughter and quiet conversations floated over to us. The cheerful sounds reminded me of happier times long past. Pain at the thought of my present miserable lot in life wrenched at me.

Digger did not stop. He checked that I was still in the cart and then said in a threatening tone, "Home Guard Indians. You try to escape from me and they'll catch you. Kill you too, no doubt."

Some children paused in their games to watch us come up, but the adults, upon seeing Digger and me, turned away. No one greeted us. As we went past their painted lodges, I saw a high wooden palisade. This was York Factory at last. Digger aimed for a large open gate. Inside was an orderly arrangement of white wooden buildings with a wooden walkway running alongside them. Directly ahead of us was another gate – this one closed. I could see buildings and sheds that formed a tidy square. I imagined a courtyard would be within. However, Digger did not go to that gate. He turned his cart to the left almost immediately, and pulled the ox to a halt. I saw him looking at the men who were bustling to and fro. There were sounds of celebration – I knew the ship's arrival was a grand occasion, since it happened only once a year and brought news and supplies with it.

There were signs that the sailors had arrived before us. Two were sprawled near the fence passing a flagon back and forth between them. One had a greyish, mud-encrusted bandage wrapped around his upper arm. The other had a similar bandage around his head. They laughed and yelled at other passersby and seemed to be enjoying themselves. They did not appear to see me.

I saw men wearing brightly coloured clothing similar to that worn by the sailors from the London supply ship: red, blue, or grey striped or checked trousers, cotton shirts and vests. Blue jackets were common. Many wore a handkerchief around their necks. Others wore furs patched together in ways unique to each coat. Some men had the leather side out, fur side in; others had knee-length coats with the fur side out. Some wore hooded white woven blankets, or had leggings made out of a woven fabric. I even saw one tall man wearing a long fur coat and carrying a brown fur cap. How I wished to have one just like it. Though it was only August, I could see my own breath as I exhaled. I watched this man as he walked along the sidewalk. He seemed to know many people, who hailed him by name as Master George. By their respectful tone, it seemed he was important. I watched him until he turned in to one of the buildings.

From ahead I heard the sounds of yelling and

scuffling. Digger turned to me and cursed. "Look at the crowd. I'll be stuck here half the night." Digger sat silent a moment, then glowered at me. "You see that trade house? You take this –" he gestured at the now bulging flour sack "– and exchange it for muskets. Short barrels. Get two. Get a box of shot and some powder. Get rum with the rest. I'll be watching, so don't try anything stupid. Now get off."

Digger made to throw me out, so I quickly scrambled over the side. I looked at a long, low, one-storey building that was inside the palisade gate. The crowd there was noisy and impatient, and I felt anxious about standing alone. I took the flour sack, however, and, mindful of the goods, carefully dragged it over to where the crowd of men stood. I saw no other woman in the queue. However, no man had troubled me aboard ship; perhaps away from Digger I would be safe.

"Well, lookee here," one grizzled man said, turning and catching sight of me. "A little wife for you, Smithy!"

The other fellow, wearing fur-lined soft shoes, turned as well. "A child," he said dismissively. "Dead before she's grown." He glanced down at the flour sack at my feet. "Get a blanket from that. I'm sick of burning dead bodies."

The grizzled man, disappointed, I guessed, at his companion's poor response, shouted hoarsely, "Hey! Lookee the wench! Must be worth a couple shillings!" Men turned and jostled each other for a look. The grizzled trader pulled at my sleeve and slung an arm over my shoulders. "What am I offered? Who wants to trade? I need some shot. A hatchet? Anyone trade me a hatchet?" I tried to pull away, to protest, but the weight of his arm and his tightening grip made that impossible.

"I'll give you a needle for her!" one man shouted. There was laughter.

"A couple of beads, how about?" shouted another. More laughter.

"A knife for her," yelled yet another. The laughter was less now; perhaps I really would be traded for a knife.

I craned my neck to see whether Digger could hear, and perhaps help. I had his trade goods, after all. He was still in the cart, glaring at me. When he saw me turn to look for him, he deliberately spat, and switched the ox. The cart moved on. Apparently the goods weren't worth much. I felt my shoulders droop. The grizzled man's shouting and the bantering replies sounded hollow and far off. I felt sick, and my head ached. I looked at my wet and cold boots and turned my face away from the smell of the man holding me tightly.

Words from a fairy tale whirled in my head, "If only your mother knew...." I could see that goose girl from the story, standing helplessly before the gate, and I felt a flush of anger sweep over me. I would not be helpless like her. I turned and jabbed the grizzled trader hard in the ribs with my elbow. He gasped, and tightened his grip around my shoulders. I said, "These are my employer's goods. He'll be here shortly."

"He'll be here shortly," the grizzled man mimicked in a high voice. His eyes narrowed. "Then what are you doing out by yourself? Trading is a man's job. Was your man kicked in the head and lost what brain he had? Maybe he just wants rid of you. Kicked you out, maybe."

"He'll be here." I tried to free myself from his arm, but he wasn't about to give up.

"You and I are waiting for trade. If he's not here by the time we're done, then maybe your trade," he waggled a stubby finger at me and the flour sack, "and my trade," he pointed to himself, "will go home together." His laughter turned to coughing and he spat a stream of brown fluid at my feet.

"Let go of me," I said, and stepped hard on the man's instep. He removed his arm, whether because of his coughing fit or my boot heel, I couldn't tell or care.

"Any valuables? Parchment beaver? Trade goods?" The man called Master George was striding alongside the crowd of men, shouting out requests. Men muttered, shook their heads, stared down at their bundles of furs.

My small victory over the grizzled man made me brave. I waved my arm and called out, "Here!" My voice carried high and clear, and I grabbed the flour sack and moved out from the crowd of waiting men.

Master George heard me. "Come on then." He looked at the grizzled man who had recovered somewhat and was reaching for me again.

"You the father?"

I shook my head.

The grizzled man whined, "Whatever is the matter, girlie? Turning on your old pop like that –"

Master George waited impatiently.

The grizzled man's companion, who until now had ignored the goings-on, backhanded him lightly on the chest. "Let her pass."

Master George shrugged and walked back towards the building ahead. Grabbing up the flour sack, I hurried after him. I went alone.

OTISEHCIKEWIYINOW – TRADER

Master George led me past a long queue of men to a large wooden building. Other men hurried to and fro, hauling goods from the York boats to the fort and back to the river for more. We came up to a broad window where a man stood inside examining furs and arguing with the man facing him. We stopped, and then Master George turned to me and said, "Oh, come inside."

When we reached a long wooden counter, Master George gestured to me to begin emptying the flour sack. He went behind the counter and sat down on a stool. He pulled a blank sheet of paper towards him and picked up a quill pen. "Well, what have you got?"

Hoping that there was something of value in the bag, notwithstanding Digger's actions, I began pulling out metal bowls, pots, knives, needles, and many other things.

"Good, good!" Master George smiled. "We'll be able to trade these back for furs. Very good."

"Thank you, sir," I said. Encouraged by his manner, I said, "I need employment. I need a place to live…I'm a hard worker."

He looked up briefly, and then turned back to the paper. "Did you come to York Factory alone?"

"Yes, sir."

"If you are old enough to come alone, then you are old enough to solve your problems. Hudson's Bay is not for the weak or faint of heart." He dipped his quill into an inkwell and carefully dotted an "i." Warming to his subject, he continued, "Too many of you poor come here, live a short time, and die. Babies die, children die, adults die. We are surrounded by death, savages, and wilderness. I can do nothing for you."

In the silence that followed, I finished emptying out the flour sack. The last item in the bag was a white woolen blanket. Slowly I pulled it out and, after a moment's hesitation, wrapped it around my shoulders. I listened to the scratching of the quill pen and the shuffling feet and murmuring voices behind me. It was quieter in the trade house than outside. And slightly warmer. I could still see the clouds of my breath, but my hands were no longer numb. Now they were burning hot, and red.

Master George picked up a cast iron pot and looked for wear. "Our Indians are very particular about their pots," the man said, by way of explanation. Satisfied it was sound, the man printed "tin cooking pot."

"It's an iron pot," I said. "It must be worth more than a tin one."

Master George paused in his calculations. "You want to dicker over prices, do you? Well, all right, an iron pot is worth more than a tin one." He drew a line through "tin," and then stopped abruptly. He looked up at me. "You know your letters! You might be of some use after all."

I turned the sheet around and read aloud names of some of the furs that had been brought in before my goods. Master George nodded curtly. The murmuring behind me grew louder and he raised his hand to show that he heard. He said slowly, "Our last clerk died this winter. We expected one to arrive from another fort in the spring, but he hasn't yet been able to leave his work. We're all short of men at present. With the ship in, it's nearly impossible to get everything done. I can offer you a place to stay and a meal a day if you'll serve till then."

As I drew breath to accept his offer, I thought of the ship I had so recently left. Would I live to return to London? If so, how would I pay for my passage? Quickly, before I could change my mind, I said, "Was the last clerk not paid for his work?"

Master George leaned back on his stool. "Were you just asking for work? Am I not offering you work? Food? Shelter? A mere chit of a girl?"

"I'll work hard. I learn quickly. I am honest. You must pay me." I was taking a risk, I knew. Surely there were sailors who knew their letters. Perhaps one of them intended to stay at the Bay for a term. Still, if nothing else, I would need passage money back to England – if I lived that long.

"A tuppence then. You'll get a tuppence a day. Whatever your name is, change it. No girl's name will appear on our accounts."

I nodded, relieved. I would not be abandoned to Digger or Dyer's plans – at least not for the moment, it seemed.

He pointed to a stool at the end of the counter. "Start now. Write down each item and fetch what I tell you. We've hardly begun to unpack the crates, but everyone wants first choice." He indicated with his head the cupboards and shelves behind him. "Don't guess what the furs are. Just write what I say and fetch what I tell you to fetch." Master George reached below the counter and brought out a handful of smooth brown objects. "These tokens go to the trader if we don't have what he wants in exchange. He can bring the tokens back and get the trade goods he wants once the ship is unloaded. I'll tell you how many to hand out. Count carefully! I'll grade the furs. If it's a Hudson's Bay Company man, then I'll tell you his name and the amount owing. We'll deduct it later from his account." He shoved the tokens back below the counter. "Now, what do you want for your goods?"

I told him.

The man laughed. "Short-barrelled muskets? You?" He looked me up and down. "Muskets are in short supply. Only our best traders are getting the short ones right now." He examined me suspiciously. "You don't want us to catch you stealing anything. It won't go well for you." He gave me some tokens. "We only honour these for a few days. With the ship in, you have no excuse not to pick up your goods. Make up your mind, or you'll not get anything."

"Thank you, sir. I will be just a moment, sir, please, before I begin?" I gestured to the outside and Master George, after a moment, said, "Ah, yes, a moment, then you may begin."

Quickly I dropped the tokens back inside the now empty bag and ran outside. Digger was no longer in his ox cart, which I saw tied to a post where he had stopped. I quickly looked around for him but he seemed nowhere easily visible. I ran over to the ox cart and began stuffing the bag beneath the cart's seat. Immediately I heard a shout. I turned to see Digger running towards me. Sheer fright made me drop the bag. Tokens began to spill out but I did not wait to pick them up. I wheeled around and raced back to the trading house, banging the door behind me without another glance in Digger's direction. Breathlessly, I went up to Master George, and took the sheaf of paper, ink, and a quill that he held out to me.

"Keep up with me now," Master George said, ignoring my gasping breath and trembling hands. "Any mistakes I'll take out of your pay. And no cheating."

I brought the stool from the other end of the counter over to where Master George sat, rearranged the blanket over my shoulders, and sat down. From that moment and for uncounted hours, I filled the sheets of paper, went for more, and filled more. I stopped looking up at the men, stopped hearing their remarks and their attempts to trick me. I concentrated on Master George's voice, handed out tokens, fetched the goods George directed me to, and ignored the noise and activity around me.

The time came when, after I handed the last twist of tobacco to the trader before me, no one stood behind him. I realized then that I hadn't seen the grizzled man. I'd been busy, and perhaps he'd been quiet. From somewhere I heard a bell toll. The front shutters and the doors closed with a bang, and Master George appeared beside me with a mug of something warm. "That's it for now. I don't suppose you can do sums?"

"Yes, my brother taught me," I said. I stretched my cramped, ink-stained fingers and then wrapped them around the warm mug. I took a long swallow. I could feel the heat as it made its way through my system.

Master George raised his eyebrows. "Your brother? Is he here?"

"He's dead," I said flatly.

"Of course," Master George said. "All the good ones die. Well, look at these lists." He pulled a stack of papers from a shelf under the counter. They were dated from July. "I want you to tot up the number of each kind of furs brought in. Your totals will be matched against the totals we have – to prevent cheating or stealing, you understand. Set it up like this," he showed me another sheet of paper, "and put your name at the top so we know who is responsible for errors."

I took a blank sheet of paper and wrote "Will" at the top.

"Will is a good choice," Master George said. "We don't have a William here at the moment. Bring those along with you to work on tonight. Now I'll show you your quarters." Master George pointed to a door at the back of the trade building. I walked alongside him while he talked. "We're backlogged. Be back here before dawn. We should be winding down soon. But there's always traders who come when the ship is due. They want the pick of the supplies. And some Hudson's Bay men don't want to wait for supplies to come to them."

"Where do they live?"

Master George stopped to look inside some of the crates the men had brought in from the York boats. "Oh," he said absently, "some are Company men from nearby forts. Others are Indians and mixed bloods who live west or south of here. They need a couple of months to reach their homes. It's all upriver from here, too, so it takes time and hard work to make the trip back. Some others don't have as far to go." He shook his head. "Normally they get goods as they bring in furs. Until we get more crates unpacked, all they buy now is trouble. Come along, now."

He walked to the end of the long building and opened a door to the outside. I followed behind. We went through the second gate that led into a large, two-storey building. Before we turned into one doorway, I caught a glimpse of an inner courtyard. I hastened to catch up to Master George, who continued to talk as we walked down a narrow corridor past numerous closed doors. "I think I'll put you in with the cook. Our regular cook died a few months ago. Freak accident, that. The bell clapper fell on his head and did him in. The bell has only recently been fixed. The girl there is filling in from the Home Guard until we get a replacement. Better you stay there. Just don't get in the way. We start early."

I smelled bread and felt a waft of almost warm air as Master George opened a narrow door. He had to duck his head to enter.

"You there!" he hollered at a woman who was

hanging a large iron kettle on a hook above a fire. She turned and wiped her hands on a leather apron. Her face was flushed from the heat. Her hair hung down her back in a long black plait. Master George walked over to her and said, "Will is working in the trading house. She'll have to stay here for the next month or so. She might need something to eat too." Master George turned to look at me. "Don't oversleep, now. The bell will ring at meal times and when it's time to work. At this time of year, with the ship in, we'll all be working long into the night. Come promptly so I can show you what you need to do."

I nodded.

"We need to regrade the furs we took in today for our records. It's a good thing many of those traders can't read," Master George said, and he laughed. "The overplus might be good this year, after all." He caught sight of flat loaves of bread cooling on a rack. He wandered over, picked one up, and then left the kitchen without another word.

I turned back to the woman, who now stood quietly beside me.

She smiled. "Are you hungry?" she asked.

"Yes," I said. "Is there something I could eat?" I was famished.

"Of course. And...would you like to...wash, before your meal?" The woman's eyes were focused on the wooden floor, it seemed. I pushed a greasy tangle of hair back from my face and felt grit and straw. Then I saw my filthy hands, whose brief contact with water at Five Fathom Hole had done nothing for them. I hated to think what my face looked like – or the rest of me.

"Please, miss," I said, my own eyes, too, suddenly finding the floor of great interest.

"This way," the woman said, and showed me to a tiny room behind the huge stone fireplace. Inside was a wooden bed with a pallet of straw. A white blanket was folded neatly on top of what I had learned from my work was a buffalo fur. On the floor beside the bed was a pair of intricately quilled leather slippers. On the windowsill were a water pitcher and a mug. The window covering was not of glass, but of a thick yellowish parchment through which fading sunlight faintly penetrated. I turned to the woman, "But is this your room?"

She shook her head. "I use it, but it belongs to the men of York Factory. I will bring you the washing basin now." I nodded my thanks, and sat down wearily on the bed.

After bathing and seeing the now-dirty wash

water, I looked with distaste at my clothing. I could not clean them, for I had nothing to wear in their stead. I sat for a moment wrapped up in the white blanket from the bed. I closed my eyes. For the first time in ages I felt warm, and dry, and safe. I opened my eyes only when I heard a quiet cough. The woman was standing beside the bed. She was holding leather leggings, a leather tunic, and leather slippers. "Would you like to wear something thicker until your own clothes are cleaned?" she said. "These may be a bit big, but they will keep you warmer than your cloth. It grows cold even now."

"Are they yours?" I asked, taking them from her and running my hands over the soft and smooth leather. "They're beautiful."

"Hardly beautiful," she said, laughing. "They are very plain – but warm. Please try them. I will help you if you have need." She showed me how to attach the leggings and tie the slippers (moccasins, she called them), and then, hefting the water basin, she left the room.

I quickly tried them on. I rolled back the cuffs on the leggings and tunic, exposing the fur. At the top, around the neck, were tiny patterns made out of some sort of quill. The moccasins were large, but there were leather laces that I wrapped around and tied to hold them securely. I draped the damp white blanket on a wooden peg to dry. Returning to the kitchen, I went to stand in front of the fire. The heat was fierce in the largest stone fireplace I had ever seen. The woman plopped something into a bowl alongside some bread and took it, a mug, and a kettle over to the table closest to the fire. She filled the empty mug. She smiled when she saw me and invited me to sit down. "Thank you," I said. "I feel so much better."

I sat down at the table and reached for the spoon. I took small cautious bites, waiting to see how my stomach reacted. After a few mouthfuls, I turned to look at the woman. "What is it?" I asked.

The woman straightened up from the fire where she was removing another tray of flat bread. She said, "The rubaboo? Onions, turnips, venison…whatever I have. Sometimes dried meat, though not as good as the pemmican we make back home."

I finished the stew and looked at my empty bowl. "But what is...pemmican?"

"Meat. Berries. Fat. Do you like the rubaboo?"

"Delicious."

I savoured the smell of bread. It reminded me

of home, before the bad times had begun. I sighed, and turned the bread over in my hands. Such a simple thing, I thought, to evoke such memories. I felt a stir of air beside me.

"Is there something wrong? I know it's not like the bread from your home."

I looked at her in surprise. The woman was looking at the fire, not at me, but no one else was in the room.

"Nothing is wrong with the food," I said. "It just reminds me of happier times."

It was her turn to look surprised. "Is that so? Me too. My grandmother always used to sing when she made bannock." The woman smiled, and brushed a strand of hair off her face with the back of her hand.

"Do you sing when you bake it?" I asked, curious.

Her smile vanished. "Few like my cooking here."

"This is the best I've eaten in months," I said. "Perhaps others have been too busy to say anything to you."

"Oh, they've said things," the woman said, frowning. She folded her arms in front of her and then said, hesitatingly, "Am I to call you Will? Is that a woman's name?"

"It's not. It's just for the records. Please call me Willa."

"A worthy name. Branches that bend, not break, in the wind. Good roots on the tree."

She meant a willow tree, I guessed. My roots, however, were dead and gone, as I would be soon. "May I ask your name?"

The woman turned to look back at the fire. "They call me Amelia in this place. My own true name is hard for your people to remember, but it means 'hare.' My mother saw one in the moon while I was being born."

"Your mother birthed you outside?" I asked. "With all the wild animals?"

"Where else?"

"A house?"

Amelia stared. "A house? You mean like this place? This is a death house. Babies born here, die here. Nothing lives. Even the animals are dead, and the trees are dead."

Rather nonplussed, I said cautiously, "I can't imagine being born outside. It must've been frightening for your mother."

Amelia laughed. "Frightening? I was the first daughter, and my mother had waited a long time to bear me. My people still speak of her dance that night."

"She danced after you were born?" I asked, scandalized. "My mother told me she was in bed many weeks after my birth. She almost died. I don't think she ever danced again after my brother and I were born."

Amelia sighed. "Yes, mothers die here." She looked down at her hands and then at my empty bowl. "Would you like more bannock? Rubaboo?"

I shook my head. The warmth of the fire and the warm meal combined to make me very tired.

"You need to rest," Amelia said.

I shook my head again. "I must go through these records before the morrow," I said.

We both looked at the thick sheaf of paper on the table. "It's very late," Amelia said slowly. "I could wake you early, when I start the morning meal. Could you work on them then?"

I hesitated. It had been such a long, frightening day. I looked at the words on the paper, and they shifted and doubled. "Perhaps you're right," I said, finally. "A few hours' sleep would be helpful."

"This way," the woman said, and we returned to the small room behind the fireplace. "Please sleep in this bed."

I was exhausted. "But where will you retire?" I protested.

The woman smiled again, and I admired the two

rows of even white teeth. There were no gaps. I had a fleeting remembrance of my father, who had refused to smile once he'd lost the last of his teeth.

"I will sleep there." She pointed to the floor. "It is warm, and I will not have to worry about falling off the bed." I looked at the floor and then back at the woman to see if she spoke in jest, but she had disappeared into the kitchen. I sighed, took off the moccasins, pulled back the fur, and collapsed on the bed.

When I awoke a few hours later, grey light filtered through the parchment. Much of the room was in shadow. I lay in bed for a few moments, thinking over the previous two days. I had to stay out of that horrible Digger's way somehow. Perhaps Amelia would know where he lived. The thought of seeing him again unnerved me. What if he tried to take me away? But he had no hold on me, had he? I wondered about the goods from the blue sack. It had seemed a hodgepodge – perhaps they had removed valuable goods and replaced them with less identifiable objects. If only I hadn't felt so lost and sick upon my arrival at Five Fathom Hole. I might have been able to avoid Digger. Seeing Dyer again was too awful to contemplate. I looked around the room. Amelia had spread the white blanket over me as I slept.

There was what appeared to be a moose robe folded in its place at the end of the bed. It was still quiet. No one else seemed awake, but I spotted my papers sitting neatly on the sill. Reminded of the work yet to be done, I hastily threw off the blanket, smoothed back my hair, and pulled on my boots. They were stiff and cold, and difficult to lace up. I already preferred the comfort of the moccasins. However, I did not want to wear out Amelia's shoes, or her kindness.

When I joined Amelia in the kitchen, she greeted me and said, "Please eat."

She handed me bannock and a thin, dry, squarish piece of something brown. "Pemmican," Amelia said. "Some of the traders bring it with them now that the berries are ripe. Would you like to try it?"

Although it looked very strange, I did not want to offend her by refusing to eat it. I took a small bite, and then another. The flavour was rich and sweet. It seemed to melt in my mouth. "This is delicious!" I told her, trying, without much success, I think, to hide my astonishment. I looked more closely at the thing. "But did you say there are berries in this? I see none."

Amelia laughed. "There are!"

"But how do you make it?" I persisted.

"Do you truly want to know?" she asked.

I nodded.

"Well, I would dry the berries, and then crush them when I pound meat of the *paskwawimostos* – buffalo meat. Then it is all mixed together with the fat. If I have the meat ready, and the time is right, then I could add fresh or dried berries without crushing them."

"Buffalo meat?" I thought of the enormous creatures I had seen in pictures. I shivered and looked around me. "Here?"

Amelia smiled and said, "There are no buffalo here."

I took another bite of the pemmican and swallowed. "Did you make it yourself? Do we partake of this often?"

Amelia shook her head. "Sometimes we make it with caribou meat. But most is brought by the traders for their return journey. For the men who remain in the fort, oatmeal porridge is their morning custom."

I ate quickly. Amelia went back to stacking bowls and utensils onto a table beside a large metal vat and then disappeared into a back room. I concentrated on warming the inkpot so it would run properly, and then set to totalling the various furs.

"More tea?" Amelia said, when she came towards me later, but her arms were full of wizened vegetables, and men were arriving for breakfast. I shook my head and rose to fill my mug myself from the kettle. Then I went back to work.

MIKI SIW – BIG EAGLE

Master George was busy filling shelves with white woolen blankets when I walked to the trade room with my bundle of papers. "You come do this," he called, when he saw me at the doorway. "Put the papers on the counter there. Did you sort them out?"

"I believe so," I said.

"Well, our senior bookkeeper has gotten a bit behind. He'll check your work soon enough."

I took the finely woven blankets from Master George and laid them neatly on the shelves. He nodded approvingly at me, saying, "That ship brought sufficient goods to tide us over for awhile. Not nearly enough, but it should stave off any violence for the time being."

He dragged over another wooden crate and peered inside. It seemed to be full of kettles and bowls. He looked back at me. "Does this look like good Brazil tobacco to you? Is that not 'tobacco' stamped on the side?"

With an expression of disgust, he put the lid back on and moved over to pry open another. "We need two ships bringing goods. No, don't put any more blankets up. Set out the beads. We've got lots now, and they take up little space. Gunpowder and shot too. They never send enough shot. Though the guns rarely hit anything, everyone wants one. Even you, eh?"

I chanced a look his way to see whether I should explain myself, but he was pondering a list and seemed not to be waiting for a reply. He set a bolt of broadcloth back in a crate and then held the papers up for my consideration. "Here's the list of goods we want, and they always send us half or a quarter of what we ask for, and never enough of the most important goods. We should send them half the furs for the orders we put in."

Master George shook his head as he hung up hatchets on nails on the wall. "We'd burst at the seams. That ship will be filled from stem to stern with every kind of fur that once walked this earth."

He walked over to another crate and pried off the lid with a hatchet. He grunted and said, "Hats. I need muskets and they send me hats."

Rummaging around in the box he came up with a knife. "Put some of these hats up. Not too many. Look for some more short knives and put them over with the beads and needles. Quickly, though – we'll open when they start banging on the door."

We both turned at the sound of knocking.

"It has to be louder than that," Master George said. "There has to be more than one or two of them out there."

I nodded and continued filling up glass jars with strings of multi-coloured beads.

When I was done, he directed me to furs that hung in one corner. "Look. These are beaver. Muskrat. Bear. Wolf. Skunk."

I repeated the names to myself after he pointed them out. I recognized the obvious ones from the day before. He showed me furs that had been damaged by traps or from being caught out of season when the fur was thin. He explained how the furs were graded according to quality and also demand determined back in England.

Master George paused for a moment, regarding me. "You don't say much, do you? Life's not so bad in the fort. Lots of food in here, and you won't get eaten by wild animals. Now, outside the fort things are different. If the hellish winter or some ailment doesn't get you, then the animals will. Or something will."

"Have you lost many men?" I asked.

"Too many. The good ones, especially. And though the Indians train our men, some still fall off a cliff, out of a boat, or get killed in some fight. Sometimes they just go off their heads. It's the lack of civilization that does it. And some are traitors or thieves – they get furs for the French pedlars. And those free men...." Master George shook his head, "Free Canadians, they call themselves, are only out for a profit for their own pocket. No company to worry about, just themselves. They can cut some pretty tough deals. They make it hard for us, but what do they care?"

Master George stretched a fur out wide and ran a hand through it absently. "We get all kinds up here these days. The pedlars, now, they have brass! They have so many trade sites, keep building more. Now they intercept our Indians, and take the best furs down south to their posts."

"Were there Free Canadians in the group we took furs from yesterday?" I was thinking about the grizzled man who had troubled me.

"No, they rarely make it this far north. Some were former servants of our Company, who set out on their own when their contracts expired. That friend of yours, that old fellow...."

I nodded.

"He used to work at a Company fort near here years ago, I think. God knows why he doesn't return to the Orkney Isles like so many others and escape the horrors of the country here. But he likely came over as a lad and so he works the territory he knows."

Well, that explained the man's background. He had obviously not been French or Indian, but I was surprised that his speech and his appearance no longer revealed his Orcadian origins.

Master George continued to explain. Perhaps he had little occasion to otherwise. "The pedlars hear from their Indian traders about what we have or don't have, and sometimes they decide to come see for themselves, stock up on our superior goods. We have done the same of course. Oh yes, we have our own sources." Master George laughed. "And we do very well for ourselves. Usually. But of late there are fewer and fewer Indian hunters. Even the Free Canadians don't come in the same numbers. And they're damned evasive about their reasons."

"Why would there be fewer of them?"

"Not worth the time, they say. Too far. Our competitors travel inland and trade with them there. The Indians then don't need to make the trip here. Indeed, some of them never have come. Some in the west don't use canoes and don't want to learn how. I don't know. You'd think they'd appreciate coming to our little pocket of civilization. Get to hear real news. I've been out there; I know what it's like." Master George paused in his efforts to pry open a lid, and looked at me. "You stand in the middle of the wilderness and can't see another man for miles. It's silent, except for the bugs and birds and wild beasts. You feel almost as if you don't exist. The trees close in on you, bushes...and then some Indian will appear right in front of you. Just like a ghost. No one's there and then one is, like magic. Ugh." He shook his head and began stacking the empty crates in a corner. "It gave me a most frightful feeling, let me tell you."

"Is Amelia an Indian?"

Master George looked at me blankly. "Who? Oh, you mean in the kitchen? Of course she is. You think white women are clamouring to come to Hudson's Bay? Knowing how long they'd likely live?" Master George shook his head. "This is no

place for a lady. Far too delicate for her to live in any sort of comfort. Everyone says so. It's a hard life. Too tough for 'em I guess." He looked over at me. "But there are many women and girls around the post. Home Guard mostly, I'd guess."

"There aren't any white women here?"

Master George laughed and said, "You seem terribly concerned about it! Well, there's always some fool who tries to sneak his family over." He paused for a moment, thinking. He continued, "There are some women living inside the fort. Mostly mixed-blood, naturally. York Factory has been here a long time, after all. Plenty of time for Company men to marry, raise a family, and bring their own grown children into the Company when the time comes. Others are full blood Natives. The men wouldn't stay without the women regardless what the governors back in London say about the matter."

I nodded and looked at the floor. Perhaps my great-uncle had family here. He had gone to some expense to rid himself of me. Perhaps he had other reasons for doing so.

Master George cleared his throat, and when he spoke his voice boomed out unnecessarily loud. "Well, don't worry. You won't be alone long. You'll get snapped up right away. Any single girl gets latched onto as soon as she arrives, no matter where she's from. Even a young lass like you. You take care. You want to last out the month, anyway." He laughed when he saw my expression at his words. "Just watch yourself, and I'm sure you'll carry on longer than that. But it's not an easy existence outside the fort, even for those born to it. Some girls just disappear. You watch yourself. Don't go outside the palisades. Too dangerous. Women just don't wander around the fort much. Too busy. Keep to themselves or travel in groups. You'll see."

The racket outside grew more insistent. Master George unhurriedly opened the broad door. Two men immediately entered and set a large crate on the floor. George walked over to confer with them. "No," he said finally, "take that one to the first warehouse with the rest; we have no immediate need for it here." It was obviously heavy, for it took them some manoeuvring before they were able to raise it again. Meanwhile, men crowded past them and swarmed up to the counter. The noise level rose and echoed in the large room. Master George gave me some paper, a quill, and some ink. He bent low and said in my ear, "Don't let them cheat you. Listen well to what I say. I'll do the weighing and the measuring. You hand out the other goods."

I concentrated on listening carefully and fetching goods quickly. After some time, the queue of men thinned. None wanted tokens, except as a counter to ensure that the number of goods they received matched the value of furs they were trading. All wanted to dicker with Master George on their furs. I grew accustomed to each man commenting on my appearance, haggling with me, and asking me to marry him. I ceased to look up at each customer. I said nothing, other than the final tally and to record what they wanted in exchange. The time came, however, when the next customer laid furs on my table and made no jesting remark. I looked up. Before me stood a young man, cleanly dressed in intricately quilled attire. His hair was long and black and held in a leather thong.

"I'm sorry, sir," I said. "You must speak to Master George first about your furs." I ran my hands over them. They were beautiful, thick, and unknown to me. "Lovely," I said, despite myself, belatedly realizing my observation would encourage the trader to barter higher with Master George. He said no word in reply. "A moment, please," I said, and went over to Master George. He was in the midst of negotiating a reduced rate for a small bale of furs in exchange for two muskets, some shot, and a bear trap. "We are short muskets, man," Master George was saying. "I know you're registered, but you've already got two for yourself. Yes, I know you've always brought us your best furs and not traded any to the French pedlars. It's a long way to come out here. I know. What is it, Will?"

"There are some furs I don't know. Good furs. He has not discussed them with you yet. I thought...."

Master George looked past me to where the man waited. His furrowed brow smoothed, and a big smile broke out on his face. He rose without another word to the trader before him and strode over to where the other man stood. "Good to see you, Miki Siw, good to see you," Master George said, beaming. He grasped the man's shoulder; the man smiled slightly and extended his hand. "You must come by for a drink – tell me where you've been, eh? Do you have some time today to stop by? For the midday meal, perhaps?"

The man nodded. "Of course. For a short time."

Master George smiled and turned to me. "This man saved my life more than once when I travelled out of the fort. He always finds the best furs, knows the best routes...look at this fur! Beautiful.

Thick, rich, smooth, not a mark on it. And this!" Master George reverently smoothed his hand over a large white fur. "Were you that near us this winter? Look at the size of this, girl. Sea bear! This'll fetch a great price." He winked at the trader standing before us. "They'll pay well for these ones, eh, Miki Siw?"

Miki Siw looked at the white fur and said slowly, "That was a healthy animal. Male. No cubs to feed."

Master George folded the furs back, one on top of the other. The abandoned trader and the other men in front of Master George's vacated stool grew restive. Master George seemed impervious to the noise as he examined each one carefully and slowly, talking all the while. I slipped behind him and took his place at the counter. "Any tokens?" I called, holding one in the air. Although there was grumbling from those in front, they made way for those with tokens. I turned, finally, when Master George came up behind me.

"You're almost through the queue, girl. Are you sure you're recording everything? What are the men asking for, anyway? You're not letting them steal anything, are you?"

I pointed wordlessly at the sheaf of papers beside my elbow and at the heap of tokens behind me, and then bent back to my work.

Master George gathered up the lists and grunted as he read. "You're quick," he said, almost reluctantly. "You go back to your spot now. We'll break for our meal soon. I – well, why don't you join us for lunch? That Miki Siw, now, he's one rare fellow, that's for sure. The stories he can tell! We'll just finish this group and then take a break. You there!" Master George yelled to a man who had just dragged a bundle of furs through the door. "Shut that door! Bar it!" Then he turned back to the men waiting. I returned to my stool.

The trading room was almost warm by the time we gathered our papers and went out through the yard towards the kitchen. "Miki's meeting me there. I see less of him each year. He doesn't like to come this far east anymore. I don't know what he's doing. Doesn't like to talk much. A pity. I have to drag out every bit of information. Not for me, mind you, but for the Company. Even so, Miki Siw has told us more about this godforsaken country – and always brings the best furs...." Master George continued to talk as we made our way down the narrow hallway past doors leading off to unknown places.

When we arrived at the kitchen, it was empty except for Amelia and Miki Siw. They were sitting opposite one another at a table, heads bent low and close as they talked.

"There you are, Miki Siw!" Master George boomed out as we entered. "Let's eat in my office. It'll get too noisy in here. Serve us in there," Master George said to Amelia, who nodded, rose from the table and began filling the bowls that she had ready on a table. The lofty piles of dirty bowls and utensils showed that most of the other men had already eaten. Amelia set three bowls on a wooden tray and turned to get three mugs. I watched while she filled one with rum and water. The other two were filled with water. Master George picked up the rum-filled one. "A tot, Miki Siw?"

Miki Siw rose smoothly from his chair, shaking his head. He picked up one of the mugs filled with water. "Not for me." He turned to Master George and said, "The sickness was bad this past season. Many died. How was it here?"

Master George stood aside while he waited for Miki Siw to precede him through the doorway. Amelia handed me the other mug, and we followed them down a narrow hallway to his office. Amelia carried the tray of food.

"Oh, not too bad," Master George replied. "We didn't have as much sickness this past winter as accidents. A few dead, of course, but not from the pox." Master George sat behind a big wooden desk and indicated to Miki Siw to sit in a chair opposite. I moved some books from a chair to the floor and sat down myself. I was no longer surprised that, with my family and our wealth gone, the rules of decorum towards me no longer pertained. While I had learned not to expect it, sometimes the little things caught me by surprise, as here, when the men sat first.

Master George continued, "That old duffer – you know, the one with the long grey plaits who used to stand at the gate each sunrise in the spring?"

Miki Siw looked at Amelia as if for confirmation, but she had busied herself handing out bowls and utensils and then withdrew quietly, closing the door behind her.

"Well," Master George went on, "one morning I went out before sunrise – I'd heard wolves howling in the night – the eeriest sound. Woke me from a deep sleep. Sound travels so far in the cold. Anyway, they seemed right outside my door. I went out, and there he was, all dressed up as if he were going somewhere special, sitting cross-legged outside the gate, just right outside. Some beautiful feathers. He was frozen stiff, though. But what a sight. Couldn't have planned it better if he'd tried. Him sitting there in the morning, facing east, the sun rising in a great big ball of flame, and there he sat, as cold as stone."

"He was one of the old ones; his children and grandchildren dead," Miki Siw said quietly. "What did you – did you bury him?"

Master George looked curiously at Miki Siw. "In the spring? Ground frozen solid? No. It was the funniest thing. I saw him there in the still of the morning, and for a minute I couldn't think what to do. I just stood as if rooted to the spot. It was quite a sight. He looked chiselled from granite. I can see him still." Master George stopped. "Finally, well, I turned to find somebody to help me load him up and she –" he gestured at the air where Amelia had been, "was right behind me. Had an armful of stuff. Then a bunch of your women appeared behind me, out of nowhere. First I was alone, and then there they all were. Well, best leave it to them, I thought. I know you have your own rituals for things...."

I watched Miki Siw's hands slowly relax and unfold. He reached for the mug of water he had set on Master George's desk, and then the bowl of stew. While we ate and Master George talked – I began to understand why he found little out from the other man – I looked around Master George's office. One wall was full of books – records of furs, perhaps, and books from England. I couldn't make out the handwriting on the spines. He had a calendar on another wall, with days crossed off. His desk was heaped with papers and folders and books.

When the men finished eating, Master George told me to get seconds. Then I returned to the kitchen to help Amelia with the washing up.

"Is Miki Siw part of your family?" I asked, while swirling water around on the bowls.

"He is my brother."

"He says very little, doesn't he?"

"He speaks when needed. And George Talk-Much says enough for two."

I laughed at the name. "I'm glad he talks to me. I'm learning from him."

"He is one you can turn away from without fear. Others must be watched."

I looked at Amelia, but her face was expressionless.

"Do you know a man – short, with a narrow, lined face. Long skinny nose. Brown hair?"

Amelia smiled wryly and said, "Most fort men look like that, *ehe?* Where did you see him?"

I told her the story about Digger and Dyer

while we finished the bowls. When I was done, she asked only, "The other man. Is there anything you remember about this one? No, not his face. Anything about the way he talked, or moved? Something you saw?"

I thought back to the other man. I spoke slowly, thinking aloud. "He spoke well. Better than the other. He seemed to be in charge. His clothes were of the English style. His shoes, though." I looked up at Amelia, excited. "He had on leather moccasins with a most striking pattern. Not like yours, but a geometric design –"

"Geometric? What is that?"

"A zigzag pattern." I demonstrated. "It was very dramatic. Black around the edges, then blue, then –"

"Red."

"Yes!" I could see them clearly in my mind's eye. I had been blessed – or cursed, depending on what I remembered – with an excellent memory. It had been very useful when my brother Charles brought home his books or taught me his lessons. So I could picture the man's moccasins, if need be, even though I had glimpsed them only briefly. "How did you know?" I asked Amelia. "Do you know him? Did you make the moccasins? His name, I recall, is Master Dyer. And his servant is called Digger."

Amelia was stacking the bowls in the shelves below the counter and didn't answer immediately. I brought a stack over to where she knelt on the floor and crouched beside her.

"I didn't make the moccasins." Amelia smiled bleakly. "You must stay away from him. Never let either one find you alone. Especially not the one in those moccasins. You must watch."

I felt the cold creeping in along my spine. "But what do you know about him? Digger is the one who took me from the ship, not the other one. And how did you know about the moccasins? Is that a common pattern?"

"Few are given that pattern. But more, it seems, as time passes. The first man you spoke of. We call him Weasel. The other, by English name of Dyer, was sent away before I came here. Now he must be back."

Her voice, normally gentle, was cold. But I persisted. I wanted to know how she knew, or what she knew. I was afraid, and I thought knowing more would ease me. But Amelia's replies grew short.

"I will tell you one thing. He has killed."

"Then why isn't he in jail? Master George told me there is one. Does no one know?"

"The people know. Your people –" she rose

gracefully, "do not care to remember. But I have warned you."

I went back to the trade room, although Master George was still closeted with his friend. The door was closed. Someone had hauled away all the furs we had taken in the morning, probably up to the curing house Master George had mentioned earlier. There were more boxes in place of the furs. I pried the lids off, and began refilling the shelves. I rearranged some of the goods so that those I handed out most frequently were in a more accessible spot. I stood on the stool and pulled down the twists of Brazil tobacco and pipes from the top shelf where they were displayed, and moved them to a lower shelf. Master George could reach them – he was surprisingly tall compared to the other men here – but he had had to get them for me whenever I had been asked for them. The rich, sweet-smelling tobacco was very popular. The woolen blankets were also an item in high demand. They had a very close weave.

I worked quickly, but my mind was on Digger and the other man. Amelia hadn't been concerned about the stolen goods, which was something I was worried about. Did they belong to a sailor who was now without? Or more likely, were these Company goods stolen from the ship? Had I done wrong to leave the tokens for Digger when, in fact, the goods weren't even his? Perhaps I should have left the tokens with Master George. I went over the problem in my mind, trying to think what I should have or could have done. Without the tokens or the goods, there seemed little I could do now to resolve it – other than try to find out more information from Master George. To whom did I owe recompense, and how would I discover that?

My thoughts turned to the other man, Dyer, and the striking moccasins he had worn. Someone had made them, and the pattern had meaning, a meaning that Amelia, and obviously others, could read. Was it the colours or the pattern? Or both? What was I to do? I could be charged with thievery, couldn't I? I could be the one imprisoned, or sent back to England to jail. I couldn't wait for them to come after me. I had to figure out a plan.

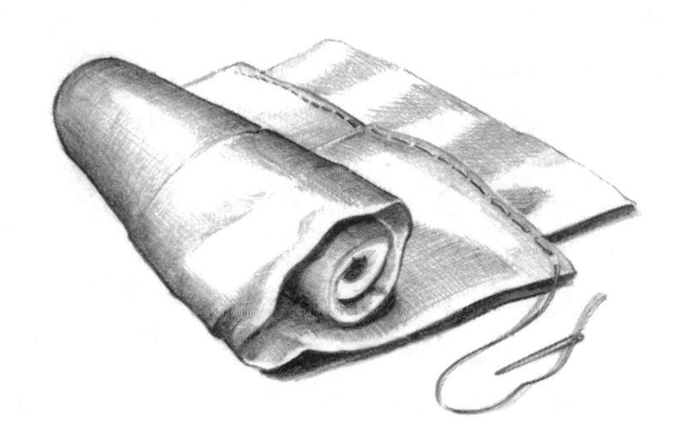

POSIHTÂSOHWINIW – BOATMAN

One morning, before Master George assigned my tasks, he went over my totals from the day before.

"We're down, again," he muttered. "Run over to the boatbuilder's, and find out when the next ones will be ready. There are complaints about the last three. Already breaking up."

He looked up impatiently as I stood uncertainly before him. "What is it?"

"I don't know where the boatbuilder is."

"You've been here a fortnight now, and you don't know where he is? What have you been doing with yourself?"

"You told me not to wander around."

Master George snorted. "And trust a girl to have no curiosity."

I had been curious and had wanted to leave the building for a change. But Amelia's warnings, my worry over the stolen goods, and Master George's remarks when I started had made me cautious. Now I wondered why I hadn't made at least some attempt. My brother might have gone out regardless. But he had also been obedient to his elders, so perhaps not. And I had been working hard, and quickly asleep most nights.

"Well, enough dreaming, there," Master George said. He put down his quill and the papers and said, in a milder tone, "I'll take you over there. Let them know they're not to bother you if they see you around. We'll do a quick tour of the fort and then you'll be able to run errands for me. Get a coat or something for over your furs." He looked more closely at my clothing. Though Master George dressed himself cleanly and well, I don't believe that he had noticed how dirty and ragged I had been when I arrived. Truly, it was only when Amelia had seen me that I became aware of it myself. The days when my family dressed in the height of fashion to attend their frequent round of parties seemed from another lifetime.

"Where did those come from?" Master George

said finally, eyes narrowed. "You didn't trade for them, did you? No, don't tell me. I don't want to know."

I ran back to the kitchen where Amelia was making bannock. Amelia had seemed disgusted with my great-uncle's coat and had not returned it to me. "Your people like these furs," she had said. "Do you see how the animal's guard hairs have worn away and only the soft pelt remains? Your people use this fur for making hats." She had held up the filthy coat and looked at it critically. "To my people its use is now gone. It should be cut up and made into winter liners for moccasins or something. This won't keep you warm in this place. I will find you a warmer coat for the cold season." She had given me a clean, white woven blanket-coat to wear in the interim, and I grabbed that from the wooden peg in our room and ran back to where Master George waited.

We walked along a wooden walkway. "To keep us from sinking beneath the muck when we walk outside," Master George explained. There wasn't much chance of that now. The earth was cold, the sky overcast, the air sharp. A thin wind blew off Hudson's Bay, hinting at approaching winter. As we walked, thick black towers of insects surrounded us and bit us in unison. I could look out from the walkway and make out certain spots so thick with insects that I couldn't see through their mass. The leather clothing Amelia had given me worked admirably – they could not bite through that, and the woolen blanket protected my head. But my hands were always itchy and sore, and it seemed impossible to keep insects off my face. Master George, after watching me ineffectually scrape a layer from my tormented brow advised, "Try not to wave your arms around so much. They're going to bite you regardless, and all that windmilling just encourages them. Be grateful you missed the worst of it."

We walked past the trading house and through the wooden palisade. There was a long wooden walkway leading down to the wharf on the Hayes River. A large building with a broad door at one end had been built to one side. As Master George directed me towards it, he told me of the important role boatbuilding was to play in the Company's future. "The ticket to beating the French," he boasted. "The boats of York will be famous one day." He guided me inside the building. There were four men inside, working in twos on two different boats. When Master George made his greeting, they all stood up quickly and answered him respectfully.

Master George walked around one large keel. "This one looks close," he observed.

"Aye. Should be ready in two more days," one man said.

"The last three Orkney boats have already served their purpose. Have you found any way to strengthen them?"

"We can make one in a fortnight, now, sir. We'll have plenty for the next season. The rapids and all the beachings give the boats a beating." He knocked on the wooden side and seemed satisfied with what he heard. "We try to keep them from breaking up so quickly, but the men don't take enough care. They seem to think they can treat them any old way and just pick up another on the way back here. But it takes time to make them."

"They're so big," I said. I walked over to a stack of oars near one man. They looked to be about twenty feet long. "How many men ride in a boat?"

The men in silence looked at Master George. "Will, my apprentice," he said, in explanation. "To replace Jackson."

The men nodded. The one who had spoken before said to me, "Six, or eight – depending."

I nodded, breathing in the fresh scent of tree sap.

"You're smelling spruce, or tamarack," the man

said. "We make the rest of the boat out of spruce planking, overlapped to make the hull watertight, then we coat it with pitch."

I pressed on the hull where the greenish-black pitch was still soft. My fingers left an imprint there.

Master George said to me, "The furs in summer come fast and furious. We don't like the traders to have to wait for an Orkney boat. Just get themselves into mischief loitering around the post. Better to get them back to their fur country."

The men nodded as one, and the first one said, "Yes, the drink is a fair strong pull. But we'll be ready for them. Now that we're past midsummer, mayhap your apprentice there could help out in her free time. She could carve oars or somelike."

I was a bit surprised at his assumption that I could be of some useful assistance other than to Master George. Never in London had I been expected to learn a useful trade. My role was to marry and retain servants to deal with the work of a household. While expectations for my brother had been higher, it was a curious feeling for me.

Master George replied, "Will is under my protection. No abusing her if she helps in her spare time." Master George turned to me. "We need these boats. If you're handy with a knife, you could help them out from time to time. If you can't help, then you can tell me of their progress. No slacking off, either. This isn't an excuse to run wild in the fort. There's enough who do that already."

"Yes, sir." Charles would envy me, if he were alive, I knew. He had loved boats, and we had spent many hours following explorers' journeys through the New World. These boats, though, flat and broad and plain, were hardly the elegant ships with the billowing sails we had seen in books.

"Does it have a sail?" I asked the lead boat-builder.

"Oh, aye, it does. Over there." He gestured to a square sheet furled around some kind of mast. "Just the one, sometimes two. But from here to the west there isn't much need for sails. Not much wind. No open sea."

Even if they weren't majestic sailing ships, I knew Charles would have been eager to help. Once I had found a slip of paper inside his favourite book. On it was written the name of a well-known supply ship to Hudson's Bay, the *Seahorse*. Its planned departure date was written below. The word "York" came after. He told me when I asked him that he intended to be on the next sailing – just after he turned eighteen. But only short months later my brother was dead.

" – have a mind to send one of the men along next trip. Show the men how to sail the boats without running them into the ground. Those French pedlars have learned how to run the canoes; why can ours not treat the Orkney boats better?"

The remarks seemed a familiar refrain, since neither Master George nor the others appeared to pay much attention. Master George was examining the hull of the boat and the others had returned to their various duties.

"Why don't your men use canoes?" I asked him timidly.

He looked up; as if surprised he had an audience still. "Have you seen one? Tried to sit in one? Like as not you'd be tipped in the water and the canoe smashed to bits just from looking at it. No, we don't like the chancy things. If it weren't for the French going inland and stealing our trade, we could wait for the Indians and other traders to come to us like always. But no, times are changing. This big, sturdy craft holds many times more than a canoe and take half the men to float her. Soon, we'll beat them at their own game. I'll wager anyone on that." The man turned back to his work with renewed vigour.

I looked around the barnlike building to outside the open doorway. It was warmer, and the sky was clearing. I could see a bit of fog still hanging about the shores of the big Hudson's Bay. The trees far away on one side were a dark, forbidding green. I walked over to the entrance and looked at the other buildings nearby. The two-storey building where I lived was the largest in the centre of the palisade. I knew already what these buildings were. There were four large bastions, or fortified large buildings, at each corner. Sheds and warehouses in between created a solid wall of buildings connecting the four main bastions to each other. The courtyard was inside this square of buildings. One large bastion at front was the officers' house. The other front bastion was the Men's house. The two bastions at rear were warehouses for furs. Adjoining buildings were the cookroom, our room, and a number of other warehouses. Master George joined me after a few moments.

"I'll take you around a bit more. Show you what to avoid and where everything is. It's not a beautiful place, but it's home," he said mockingly.

We headed back up the wooden walkway and George indicated which buildings were which.

There was an oil shed, a cask room, a coopers' shed, a blacksmiths' shed, and a meat shed. On the other side of the main building, "Old Octagon," Master George called it, were the men's winter dwellings, the carpenters' shed, another fur shed, a shop house, a keg shed, and, in the far back corner, a large distillery. Within a smaller palisade were another cookroom and a winter house. One small building farther away from the rest was made of stone – the magazine, Amelia had told me, where ammunition was stored.

"How many men work here?" I asked Master George.

"Oh, must be about sixty-five or so, including the labourers and officers. Then there's the Home Guard help. Including the women and girls you're so concerned about, there must be two hundred or more people here at peak season." He waved in the direction of the palisade. "Usually everyone isn't all here at the same time, however. They might be out cutting wood, hunting, what all. Still, it can get crowded. Food can become scarce. People get hungry. There have been too many winters when the cooks are scraping the barrels for flour."

There seemed all of two hundred men inside

the fort now. I pulled the white hood closer to my face. If Digger or Dyer saw me, they might be able to take me away, or even accuse me of stealing. Who knew what they might be capable of?

"When I arrived here," I ventured as we walked along, "I saw a man. He was called 'Digger.' He –"

Master George snorted and said, "Digger is a handy name for him. He digs graves on our one day of summer and then fills them with bodies the rest of the year. You'll see him again. He gets goods from the dead as partial payment, you might say, for the trouble. He's always in, trading bits of this and that. Troublesome chap, though. Stay away from him. He's one who pulls the demon out of the rum." We walked a bit farther in silence. Then Master George pointed to an area in one corner of the palisade where yellowed stalks and uprooted vines lay withering. Dandelions grew wild. Most of their heads had turned to seedy fluff and blown away.

"There's where the seeds are started when the ground thaws. Perhaps you could help with the planting in your free time next season, if the soil hasn't blown away to the sand below. We haven't had much success in past years, but then the growing season is short. And when it needs attention, we're smack in the middle of trading season. Not that those in London will believe it."

"We had gardens at our home. Are there any livestock?"

"A farmer too, are you?"

"No, sir. Others tended them."

"Well, you've seen the cows. A hardy Orkney stock. Pigs sometimes come. We were expecting one to arrive on this ship, but it met up with the cook, I'm told. The annoying creatures break fences and eat what little produce we have, and if they don't run off, then they barely live through the summer."

"Why not?"

"There's not a great deal for them to eat. And they like to eat."

"What crops do you grow?"

Master George laughed. "I wouldn't call them crops. We get a few vegetables on occasion. Turnips are bad as often as not. We get a few spindly beans and peas if we're lucky and if they don't rot in the pod. We've had rather good luck with the dandelions, though. Makes a refreshing salad come spring."

"I presume the berries in the pemmican grow near here."

"I suppose so. The Home Guard Indians take

care of it for us. Mind you, that's for the traders on their journeys. We don't eat much of it anymore in the fort. No need with the annual supply ships coming. If they miss coming again, though, then of course we must be prepared for it."

After the tour we made our way back to the trading house. The bell sounded loudly. Master George pointed out the bell tower before we entered the trading house. "I'm sure you've seen how the bell keeps us punctual and civilized. We have schedules here that must be followed."

There was a gathering of Hudson's Bay Company men before the doors, which were open. They were hauling crates to the warehouses where the goods would be repackaged into smaller quantities for shipping to the other forts. We went in by a side door.

"Go have your midday meal, then meet me at my office."

I nodded and turned to go.

"And Will. The man you mentioned, Digger. He is servant to another man in the Company. A man by the name of Dyer. Dyer is expected here from another fort this month, although I imagine he's lurking in the vicinity already. He is a Company surgeon, however, and so we must endure his vexatious presence. Still, try to stay out of his way. Digger, while troublesome, does have his uses; Dyer does not. I hope you haven't gotten into some sort of trouble so soon. I can't abide treachery. Take heed."

SHEDDING MOON: SEPTEMBER, WHEN THE DEER SHED THEIR HORNS

Too soon, the supply ship and the traders were gone. We were no longer busy morning until night packing and recording last-minute furs for the trip to London, tallying goods, recopying accounts for the London governors. The queues, the hectic pace of always washing utensils, preparing meals for the Hudson's Bay Company men, and collapsing, exhausted, into bed at night – all these things came suddenly to an end.

One day I looked up from my stool in the trading house and there was nothing left to count, sort, or pack. I sat for a moment and listened. I heard the faint sounds of geese outside, readying themselves for their winter migration. I shivered, thinking about the horrors I had heard from the men in the fort; about the screaming winds and snow so deep a man could step outside the fort, fall into a drift, and not be found until spring. I put down my quill pen and set off for the kitchen, where Amelia was clearing away the last of the midday meal.

She looked at me and smiled. "You've come back to yourself," she said.

"There is nothing needing immediate attention. I had a moment to think." I helped myself to some of the still-warm bannock. "I heard some geese outside."

"They're late leaving."

"At least the mosquitoes are gone." I scratched my head. They had been so thick that at times it was hard to breathe. The incessant hum of insects looking for a square inch to bite put us to sleep at night and woke us in the morning. Although Amelia had given me gauze netting to hang over the bed, some were invariably trapped inside with me. Amelia said they didn't bother her too much, and she did seem to get bitten less than I. Certainly the bumps and welts I experienced she did not. She did, however, make up an onion salve that reduced the itching and the pain, and it was a great comfort. I had noticed that some of the traders came in coated in a thick grease that was supposed to keep the insects from biting, but when I asked Master George about it, he just laughed, and said, "Will, it's not to be contemplated."

After the ship left Five Fathom Hole, the days settled into a regular routine. As I grew more familiar with my work, I was able to accomplish more. Amelia and Master George both told me there was no need to rush. I was to make sure the work was done well, not necessarily quickly. We have all winter, Master George told me, almost grimly. But I found that the more familiar I became with the work required, the more time there was to remember England, and my family, and all that had gone before.

I started to help Amelia in the servants' kitchen when Master George didn't need me. Since the ship was gone, some of the Company men had gone back to preparing their own meals in their own areas. Most, however, who disliked their own cookery, continued to drop by the kitchen where Amelia portioned out the men's allotment. There they would demand that she prepare them a pie or some porridge. When she did this once or twice, a few other men came by with the same intentions. Soon, there was a large group of regulars who came by when the bell rang to signal meals or work times. Digger appeared at one of these meals and I nervously pointed him out to Amelia.

"He and Dyer have been stationed down at Five Fathom Hole while the ship was loaded and unloaded; that's why you haven't seen them until now," Amelia explained. "All help is needed then – even theirs – and those two are happy for any chance to handle ship goods."

Digger didn't approach me, however, and I certainly made no attempt to speak to him. The other man, Dyer, did not appear. I prayed I would never be ill if he were the only surgeon. I also didn't know what had happened to my own bag. Was it lying abandoned at Five Fathom Hole?

Since Amelia had given me warm clothes, I had hung the woolen blanket I had taken from the blue bag up on a peg in the trading room and pinned it open. I hoped in this way to have the owner recognize it, although there were many blankets like it in the factory already. Amelia told me she had heard no complaints of missing belongings that matched the goods I had traded. Very likely George would come across missing Company goods when inventory was completed. Since I was helping him with that, I would be able to see if the goods were missing from the London supplies, and perhaps have George deduct their value from my pay packet. If they weren't listed, then perhaps the goods were Dyer's or Digger's, and they were merely trading them in. I thought that unlikely, however. There were men searching for a gold sword sent for some important officer at another fort that had inexplicably gone astray, but not much else of significance.

Always, Amelia said, belongings went missing every time a ship arrived. In fact, so many boxes were mislaid that men at the fort had grown resigned to the inevitable "slippage," as they called it. Some insisted certain items had never made their way offshore from England or the islands, but no one knew for sure.

A week later I watched some of the men arrive for their midday meal. Amelia was making meat pies, and word had gotten round. Men had brought in their flour and other rationed food items and asked her to prepare pies for them as well. There was quite a large group – even some of the officers had appeared in the common kitchen, although they had their own kitchen and cook with jealously guarded entrance privileges. Although the men had been issued their food rations and were to cook meals in their own mess now that the ship had gone, Amelia thought it more sensible to continue preparing certain food for the men rather than have each prepare his own meal from the raw ingredients. "They don't prepare it properly; many get sick from their own cooking," Amelia explained. The men didn't care why she cooked for them and many were more than happy to have someone take over the job.

Following Amelia's example, I had wrapped my thick blanket over my head and shoulders. The days were getting shorter; the sun had begun to stay below the horizon for a good part of the morning. When a wind blew off the Hudson's Bay, I was reminded that winter unlike any I had spent in England, was on the way. The blanket would keep me warm and, almost as important to me, would shield my face from the others.

While there was a great deal of shouting and scraping of chairs, I did not see Digger until near the end of the meal. When he walked in, I noticed no one greeted him; no one seemed even to notice him. I edged back into the shadowed corridor until he had been served. He sat down alone at an empty table. He ate quickly. A few minutes later, the other man, Dyer, entered from another door. There was a curious hush. As sometimes happens, for no particular reason, conversations ended simultaneously and, in the space of silence, men looked up, saw Dyer, and quickly looked away. Conversation began again, shocking in its sudden noise. Amelia turned to look at me, her lips in a tight line. I backed up once more and stepped on someone's foot.

"Frightened of all the commotion?" Master George was behind me, and he gave me a push forward. "Have your meat pie. I've got errands for you to run, and you won't have time to eat later." His voice, always loud, seemed now to boom and echo around the large room.

I stared at the floor, pulling the blanket closely around my face. "I've eaten, thank you; I can do your errands now."

Master George took me by the arm. "Then come sit with me while I eat, and I'll tell you what needs doing."

I followed, my legs feeling numb. I waited silently beside him, staring at the rough flooring boards while Amelia filled his bowl. Men called to him to sit at their tables, but he waved them off. Then I saw the startling moccasins appear alongside mine. I turned my head and followed Master George's back. He went to Digger's table.

"Sit down, sit down," Master George said to me. I sat opposite Master George and fixed my eyes on his bowl. I heard the chair beside Master George scrape the floor and I knew who was the fourth at the table.

"Got yourself a bit of flesh, have you, George?"

"Greetings to you too, Dyer. I'd heard you were back," Master George said mildly. Dyer sat down and I heard the clinking of utensils.

"This is Will, my apprentice servant. Sent over from London. You know how short-handed we are, don't you, Digger?"

"Yes, sir. For certain we are."

Master George picked up his steaming mug, and the smell of rum wafted over to me. "Bad time of year to be short-handed. Will here is learning the trade."

"London is hard-pressed if they've taken to raiding orphanages to supply apprentices to us here," Dyer said, in a regretful tone.

Master George set his mug down and picked up his fork. "Sometimes those with a better pedigree just don't seem able to succeed. Sometimes I wonder why they stay, when there is so little in these wilds to offer them. Take youngsters, though, say from bad situations, and send them here – well, they're used to hard times and to the lack of the niceties of life. They don't miss what they've never had, isn't that correct, Will?"

I nodded, and thought about how little I missed the niceties of life we had had as a family, before my father's business losses and the subsequent deaths. I had lost far more than niceties.

There was a pause while the three men ate.

Then Dyer spoke. "The trouble with these orphans, however, is the need to watch them. They might pick up things that don't belong to them."

Master George smiled and said, "Will here isn't foolish. Digger, now, I haven't seen you for awhile. Say you showed up suddenly, with some goods when nobody had died; well, then we'd have reason to wonder. But Digger's too clever for that, aren't you, Digger?" He pointed his fork at Digger's face while he addressed Dyer. "They may come from poor families, Dyer, but that doesn't mean they're completely stupid."

Dyer forced a laugh. "Just a friendly warning, George. You never know what the lower classes will be plotting."

"Will knows on which side the bread is buttered. The lower classes don't come here from pleasant circumstances. Even working here is better than the poorhouse or jail. And I'm sure everyone here knows the punishment for thievery from the Company."

Again there was silence. Then Dyer said, "When is your next furlough to London, George? You must be counting the days?"

It was George's turn to laugh, uncomfortably, it seemed. "A year yet. There has been a delay because of the personnel problems."

"And you're staying on because of it." Dyer leaned back in his chair and crossed his legs. "It's easy for them to command our lives like pawns on a board. There they sit, drinking rum in their leather-bound offices, getting rich, while we die out here in this frozen wasteland."

"They don't force you to renew your work contract, Dyer," Master George said, although his hand had tightened around his mug.

"And go back to what?" Dyer said bitterly. "That small legal matter hangs round my neck like a stinking albatross. No, I'll endure one more term, and by then all will be forgotten and another man will be at the centre of hysteria. Then I'll be able to inhabit my quarters in peace."

"And in wealth, no doubt."

"Indeed."

Silence fell once more. Around us the chairs were empty, and Amelia was clearing the tables.

Master George sighed and peered into his empty mug. He looked up at me and his expression changed. "Time to earn your keep, Will; come along. Good day, Dyer. Digger."

Hastily I stood and pushed in my chair while the two men said good day. I followed Master George out of the kitchen and into his office. He pulled out his chair and sat behind his enormous desk, and I sat on a chair opposite. He sat silently for a moment, rubbing his chin absentmindedly. Like Dyer, he was clean-shaven. Then he opened a desk drawer and pulled out some papers.

"This is a contract," he said. "It's time you signed one. You seem to be reliable, and you learn quickly and well. This says you will stay with the Company for five years, after which you will be free to go on your way. What do you say?"

I took the contract from his hands. I didn't know what to say. I had not been looking to the future, merely working through one day and then the next. Was there any reason to sign? Was there any reason not to?

"I thought you didn't hire girls."

Master George shrugged. "Nowhere in there does it ask whether you're lad or lass. We will keep your name as William, though. You'll get a bit more money than before, though there's little enough to spend it on. You stay here instead of going to London and you could make yourself a very nice living. You marry, however, and of course you would not be able to work here or collect a wage. It's up to you."

I had no intention nor any thought of marrying. Moreover, planning for the future was a curiously new feeling. I had been plodding along, feeling that I had somehow been overlooked and would soon join my family in the grave. But here I remained. If I wasn't here in five years, then no matter. If I was here, then I might as well have a job and some money to look after myself. I signed the form.

Master George, to my surprise, smiled broadly. "I'll let it be known you've signed on with the Company. It will help you get along."

I nodded. Master George gathered up some papers and then pulled out a journal listing the stock and the trades. We spent the next few hours poring over the documents and comparing past sales figures. It was slow, detailed work. By the time we finished it was late. The chill in the air was noticeable, and we quickly made our way back to the kitchen.

TAKWÂKIN – FALL

Now that the busy season had ended, Master George told me I could spend the latter half of the Sabbath Day on my own. I finished my midday meal and wandered into the sleeping quarters to look for Amelia. I had asked her to teach me words for the seasons in one of the many languages she spoke, and I would practice them while I worked. She began to teach me Cree words, thinking it might be useful for me, since the language was spoken widely. It was an interesting way to pass the time. On this day she was sitting near the parchment-covered window, her quillwork lying untouched in her lap.

"Do you miss your family?" I ventured.

She turned at my words. Then she picked up her quillwork and a bone needle and began the intricate task of patterning and attaching the quills to the leather. I sat down on the bed and watched her work.

"I try not to think of them."

"Do they ever visit you?"

"My brother, sometimes, as you know. My mother, no. I have not seen or spoken with her since I've come here."

"And how long have you been at the fort?"

"I've been working with the Home Guard for three summers. This is my first season working within the fort."

"Is your home far away?"

"Not far enough. There is not enough earth between this place and the rest of the world."

I was silent. Amelia spoke without bitterness, seemingly matter-of-fact. She tipped her work away from herself and studied it critically. I saw she was quilling around a leather basket lid. In the centre was the faint tracing of a hare, her favourite choice of design. She had worked the quills in a delicate pattern of blue, green, and white. The circular container was already entirely quilled. Tiny hares leaped along, following the seasons; one portion had a brown hare leaping through tall green grasses; another was of a hare reclining by water and mountains; turning the container again showed a hare beginning to turn colour, bounding gracefully over red and gold leaves; and last was a white hare, the quills their natural colour and the blacker tips artfully attached so that the darker ends formed the animal's eyes and claws. The top and bottom edges of the container were rimmed in tiny hares; all white along the bottom and all black along the top.

Amelia continued, "I hope I do honour to the family. But my mother never comes here. I am her only daughter. Perhaps I am not walking the right path."

"What do you mean? Which path?"

"I am here to learn about your people. Your different customs and your…" she gestured apologetically, "different ways. Perhaps we can live together in this land."

I thought of the wars we English had fought with France. I thought of my own family and all our differences.

"Do you think so, really?"

She laughed quietly, and this time bitterly. "We must try."

"Did your mother send you here to learn?"

"My mother does not send me here or there.

We talked about it, all of us, and when the talk turned to sending me, I agreed. I saw my mother about to speak. Perhaps she felt I could not carry such a burden. I was a girl of fifteen when I came here. But she did not speak. Many girls have been..." Amelia hesitated, then said, "many have returned changed, or they don't return at all. But I am strong. I have been here many seasons. And soon I will be back with my people."

"You've learned what you came for?"

"Some small amount. And I will be home at next shedding moon."

"You must be very excited about that."

"I try not to think about it too much. If I do, the days do not pass."

"Won't it seem strange to leave York Factory after so long?"

Amelia looked at her hands and sighed. "It will be wonderful."

I shivered. "I don't understand how you could live out there in the wilds. All those vicious animals, the cold, other...strangers wandering around. It must be very dangerous. Many people must die. And how do you find food in the winter?"

"The 'wilds' as you call it is the natural world. This place is not natural. It smells. It is hard to breathe with so many men crowded together.

There are so few women here. It is so strange."

"Do you have any sisters?" I asked.

"No. Only Miki Siw, my brother. But I have grandmothers and aunts and cousins."

"Where is your father?"

Amelia smiled again and said, "He is a spiritual man. He sees many things before they happen. He will be in retreat now. He goes every year to a place full of spiritual presences, where our ancestors have always gone." She touched my shoulder. "What of your family? How is it that you are here alone, like me?"

For a moment I couldn't get the words out. I cleared my throat and said, "They are all dead."

Amelia looked shocked. "Your whole clan? And only you were spared? Was it a sickness?"

"My father lost our family fortune. We had to leave our home. My father – was ashamed. He killed himself." I could hear the bitterness in my voice. "The rest of us, my mother, my brother, and me, tried to go on as best we could. But we had little money, no shelter. There was a plague in the city, and we couldn't afford to leave. Then my brother became ill. My mother nursed him until she sickened as well. My brother was barely in the ground when my mother followed him to the grave. And here I am."

"But where was the rest of your family? Your aunts? Your cousins? Could no one help you?"

"My great-uncle assisted me. He bought me passage on this ship."

"But he did not come with you?"

"No. Sometimes I wonder if he sent me here as punishment – he was outraged at my father, and there was no one else to pay for my father's sins."

"Sending you here is one thing. But sending you here alone, to this place, without any family?"

"You're here alone."

"But I chose to come here."

"That's true. And that ship!" I shuddered and pulled the fur on the bed around my shoulders.

"When our people go on those ships, they die," Amelia said soberly. "And when I see your ships unloaded here, many look as though they want to die. That is a terrible way to live."

"Terrible," I agreed. Still, the last few months in England had been so wretched that my life before that time seemed like a dream. I looked down at my leather clothes and around the tiny room in which Amelia and I sat, and I shook my head. "Life is so unpredictable."

"It's difficult, sometimes, to see a pattern."

"Your mother. You have said she is a healer?"

"My mother is many things. One of those things is her knowledge of healing. I have been learning from her since I was a small child. There is much to know."

"My mother wanted to be a herbalist, which is a healer, in a way. But my father did not approve and would not let her." I still could not think for long about my mother. A mere whisper of her name in my mind could bring the black dogs of misery. I didn't want to have my memory of her linked to such an absence of hope.

"Wouldn't let her? How strange! The white men here are so funny. They make noises when women carry heavy loads and pull sleds, yet women are so strong, and we do it well. Why should they tell us what to do?"

"You're not as strong as men."

"No," Amelia said. "We're stronger. Our people refuse to journey without women; for without us to do the heavy work and carry supplies, no man could travel anywhere far. Not without great trouble."

I almost laughed. How could she say such a thing? Yet I recalled seeing her heave the gigantic soup pots and sling heavy fur bales onto her back as though they weighed nothing. For all that she was so slight, she did seem very strong.

Amelia bent over her work again. "Every spring is hard because I think of what my family would be doing. Winter is horrible because the whole world seems frozen, and I'm frozen in this place with dreadful drunken men. The time passed much more quickly when I first came. Now each day seems to last a season." She sighed and set her work down. "I must get out of the fort. Why don't you come with me? We'll look for the last of the greens and berries."

Gradually, over the past few weeks, I had left the buildings with Amelia to wander far over the barren land. I nodded. "I must check with Master George to make sure he doesn't need me for something."

"George is a good man," Amelia said, approvingly, "though often he does not see very far. Still, he watches out for you and one has to like him for that."

"Master George looks for me to give me work," I said, laughing. "Although sometimes he does supervise me as a father might."

"An elder brother, perhaps. He is but twenty-four seasons, after all."

I was surprised. "He seems much older than that," I said.

Amelia knelt to retie her moccasins. "He tries

to act older so that the men will listen to him." She pulled on her blanket and adjusted it around her face. "Of course, having a big presence and a loud voice help, too. I'm ready. Shall I meet you at the main doors?"

"Yes that would be fine. I'll be as quick as I can."

I walked swiftly over to George's office. The door was open and I saw him sitting at his desk, staring straight ahead – at what, I couldn't see – his hands around a mug.

I knocked softly at the door and he started.

"Eh?" he said. "Oh, it's you, Will. Yes?"

"I would like permission to look for greens with Amelia outside the fort."

"Greens in this godforsaken country? Now?" George took a swallow from his mug. "Go ahead. Don't be long. You know how quickly darkness falls these days."

I gave my thanks and ran to meet Amelia. Leaving the walls of the fort, though it was mere wood holding us in, always seemed dangerous. Yet Amelia seemed to think it was safer outside the walls than in.

Amelia had a bark sack on her back, and she held out another to me. I struggled to put it on; for all its size, it was lightweight and pliable, and once on I forgot it was there.

"Did you make these?"

"There are no birch trees here. One of the Home Guard brought them to me."

Amelia and I walked past the garden – Amelia and I had dug up potatoes half the size of a hen's egg and picked wizened turnips and beans that had struggled weakly through the summer. More cattle had been promised for the following year, though George said it annoyed the London governors that the cattle must be sent each year – but better to eat them than watch them die of starvation.

We headed through the gates, and I waved at one of the boatbuilders. I often dealt with them – taking them drinks or small supplies if they ran short – if I happened to be within hailing distance. We wandered over to where some of the Home Guard were readying themselves for a trip to more moderate climates. Some had stayed longer than was safe. Amelia said they might die on their way home.

The Home Guard lodges were far fewer than when I had arrived. Most of the colourful ones had disappeared – perhaps taken by their owners who had left the area. Some women and children who remained were busy building lower, more dome-shaped dwellings, and covering them with skins that still retained their fur. The ground inside was dug down a foot or so to provide more headroom and protection from the cold and winds. I could easily understand how these changes would make for a warmer home over the winter.

"Many of the Home Guard have returned to their homelands," Amelia explained. "There is not enough food or work or reason for them all to stay through the cold time. In bad years some bring the sick or elderly or starving ones to the fort, but otherwise few stay."

"They guard the fort? From whom?"

"Not just guarding anymore. They used to protect the Hudson's Bay men from their enemies, but that was long ago. They now work hard at other things. They provide your meat and fish and firewood all winter, for instance. For those who stay, it is a fierce life. The rest will return when the ice goes from the rivers. And when the other traders come with the furs, there will be someone to interpret or help with the unloading or repairing of all the things that break or need to be redone."

The sun had burned off much of the fog that frequently hung in the dark scrub. The sky was a pale grey. I was struck by the silence, the calmness. Almost without noticing I had become accustomed to hearing men shouting and carousing, the clang and clatter of men eating and drinking, muskets and other guns blasting at birds and other creatures day and night. Thin clouds trailed across the sky, and cries of birds swimming in the marshes and rivers filled our ears. The air, even in mid-afternoon, had a bitter edge.

When we drew close to one lodge, Amelia called out a greeting. A woman turned. When she saw Amelia, she smiled, put aside the moccasin she was working on, and stood up, dusting off her hands on her leggings. After glancing at me, she took Amelia's hands in hers and looked closely into her face.

"You were right. They got to them in time. Many would be dead without your help. Excuse me," she said, turning to me, "my English is not good. Could I talk in my tongue?"

That she should think to ask me, a stranger, for permission, took me by surprise. Since my family had died, no one else, other than Amelia, had shown any concern for what I might wish. "Of course," I said.

She invited us back to her fire, where we knelt beside her on the ground. She poured us each a cup of warm sweet tea, and then proceeded to speak very rapidly to Amelia. I looked at the activity around us. After the drab walls of the fort, the vivid colours struck me once again – on tents, clothing, and blankets. A mother walked past us with a baby swaddled and attached to a pack on her back. From the hood on its head to the underside of the pack, all was intricately embroidered or worked with dyed quills. Of all the people present, Amelia and I were the most plainly dressed. I watched the small children who remained, and was reminded of my own family and my former life. One little girl sat near a cozy looking lodge, head bent over a heap of leather, aiding in preparations for winter.

I felt a touch on my sleeve, and turned back to Amelia and her friend. "Willa, this is Saskwatoomina. She is a friend of our family, and brings me news."

Saskwatoomina smiled at me again and said, "How do you like this land?" I looked at the desolate stretch of land and the broad grey sky and felt the damp chill in the air. Involuntarily, I shivered and said, uncomfortably, "I haven't seen much. However, it seems rather…empty."

She laughed heartily. "*Ehe?* We are lucky for that."

Unlike Amelia, who spoke English like one

born to it, I had to listen carefully to Saskwatoomina's words. She glanced sideways at Amelia, who had begun to sort dried peas or beans or something similar from one wooden bowl to another.

"Can I come pick...greens?"

The three of us rose and I brushed off the bits of dust and stones that clung to my leggings. When we turned, an older boy stood, waiting to be noticed by Amelia. When she saw him, she broke into surprised laughter and quickly went to him. She spoke rapidly to him in another language and his face broke into a smile, but it vanished when he turned to look at me. It was plain he felt constrained by my presence.

Amelia ignored his reaction. "Willa, meet my cousin, Kino Sesis."

I made my greetings.

Amelia continued, "His name means 'small fish' because once when he was a child he wandered off. We searched for him until we had no hope left. As dark fell, he walked back to our camp, a string of fish over his little shoulder, puzzled by all the cries and cheers when we saw him. He couldn't get lost, he said. He knew where he was all along. We've called him 'small fish' ever after. Though, as you can see, he's grown since then."

Kino Sesis smiled briefly at the story, despite his apparent desire to scowl in my direction.

Saskwatoomina took my arm in hers and said, "Let's go before dark." Amelia and the boy followed behind. I could hear his voice murmuring continuously to her. From the urgency with which he spoke, I did not think it was merely casual conversation. I listened hard for Saskwatoomina's soft voice as she spoke to me, punctuated by the increasingly sharp tone of the boy's voice. Obviously, Amelia and he disagreed about something.

Saskwatoomina led us to a marshy area where dried brown stalks grew in thick bunches. Pushing a thatch of them to one side with her arm, Saskwatoomina pointed to the pale green stalks that had sprung amongst them. "These are very good to eat after a long dark winter. And these." She plucked out another grasslike stem with a small white bulb on the end and handed it to me. I caught the pungent smell of onion. Images of the annual Christmas feast flashed through my mind, with the bread and onion and savoury pies and pheasant. The smell of marsh was strong. I picked some onions and put them in the birch bark packsack. Saskwatoomina already had an armful. She walked over to me and dumped hers on top of mine.

"That should do for now," Saskwatoomina said. "Let's see if we can find something else good to eat."

I nodded, but shivered involuntarily. The ground and the plants were icy. My hands already felt frozen.

"You are cold?" Saskwatoomina asked me, seeming surprised. "It will get much colder. You must dress warmer, I think." She moved away from the marsh and headed upland. "We will find berries instead," she said. "They are warmer to pick."

Mystified by her remark but curious, I followed her, pulling my hands up inside the furry sleeves of my tunic. We walked along, passing rocks scattered here and there that were crusted in circles of a brilliant orange or a dull grey-green lichen. Saskwatoomina named an animal that she said loved to eat lichen and, when I expressed my puzzlement, she waggled her hands over her head, imitating some antlered animal and said "*atihk*" or "*xalibou*," the deer-like creatures that ran in herds through the land. We also passed a few wretched looking specimens of trees; very old, Saskwatoomina told me solemnly, and I stared in amazement at them. They were barely as tall as I, and I could easily span their trunks with one hand. Compared to a tree in the countryside back home, one would have thought these were dying seedlings, but Saskwatoomina insisted they were not.

Occasionally I turned to see if Amelia was near; I was anxious about getting too far from her and York Factory, but she and the boy were following along behind us, each intent on the other. Every so often, one or two other people would approach them and talk to Amelia, then leave, but the boy always remained.

We reached an area where a dense mass of leathery looking plants blanketed the ground. Amelia and I had continued to gather plants and berries, as we had since the traders had begun to leave the fort. Already the few flowers were no more. The bright splash of berries too was no longer common; many had been picked by humans or animals. Only occasionally did we now come upon some, most often one Amelia called crowberry, with purplish black fruit full of large hard seeds. Amelia had told me that while there were fewer flowers and plants here than in places farther away, still there were some fine ones in the spring.

"Here," Saskwatoomina, pointed, "pick these, and tell me if you still feel cold after."

I crouched down hesitantly beside her and eyed the few remaining black and red berries, which grew more abundantly here than elsewhere. "Are they safe to eat?" I asked her.

Saskwatoomina laughed and said, "Would we pick them if they were not?" She picked a handful of red ones and popped them in her mouth. "Mmm," she said and patted her stomach.

I looked back at Amelia; she crouched down a few yards away among the masses of plants and was picking berries also, head down, while the boy stood talking beside her.

I reached towards the plants and began to pick. The plants and berries were warm on my fingers, perhaps because they were so close to the ground and densely packed.

The boy's voice again cut through the air. It was controlled but vehement. Saskwatoomina glanced at me to see if I'd heard, but just as quickly she remembered that I couldn't understand. I turned to watch the boy as he waved an arm contemptuously towards the fort, and then waved it in a wide arc towards the Home Guard, but he had lowered his voice. Amelia spoke in a soothing tone, but he stood with his arms folded, looking away from her.

"Come," Saskwatoomina said, touching my arm, drawing me away from the two. "We'll go to the fire, *ehe?*"

Once back at the camp, sitting close to the flames, I watched as small children edged nearer and nearer to where I sat. Older children stayed at a distance, but watched me nonetheless. In fact, when I turned to look, people were watching me from everywhere; except that the adults were a bit more discreet about it. Noticing my sudden discomfort, Saskwatoomina said, "We hardly ever see a white woman this far north. That's why children look at you – but they mean you no harm."

I saw Amelia coming back. The boy was gone, but others were with her, talking intently. The darkening sky and cold and all the strangers were making me nervous. I wasn't used to sitting outside, and I felt vulnerable and exposed.

I didn't feel reassured when Amelia touched my arm and said urgently, "We must go. Quickly, get your bag and we'll return to the fort."

I had time to notice only that Saskwatoomina was busily stuffing Amelia's birch sack full of onions and berries, handing it to Amelia, and then we were hastening back to the fort.

"Do they shut the gates at a certain time?" I asked.

"Yes, they do, but we have time yet." Amelia said absently.

"Is something wrong? Is your mother well?"

"I hope she is well. No one here has seen her recently."

"But your cousin…."

Amelia glanced at me as we reached the back entrance to our quarters. "Yes, Kino had some trouble. He does not want to wait for us."

As we entered the fort, a man came reeling out from nowhere and grabbed Amelia's arm.

"C'mere, sweet, let's visit a spell." The reek of alcohol fumes surrounded him.

I jumped back involuntarily, and Amelia, in an overly loud voice said, "Time to eat. We must get your food ready." She shook the sack of onions in his face and then pulled her arm away from him.

He overbalanced in his effort to hang on to her and caught a whiff of onions, which seemed to steady him for a moment. He peered at her, trying to focus his eyes. "Cook, are you? Oh, well. Might as well eat."

Amelia quickly moved ahead of him and we slipped inside the fort.

I let out my breath. "I wasn't expecting that. Is that all some of the men do, just drink?"

Amelia didn't answer. When I looked at her, her lips were tight in a line and her forehead creased. "Soon," she muttered to herself, "soon I will be home."

ÂYIMIPAYIWIN – HE GETS HIM INTO TROUBLE

Looking for Master George the next morning, I found him in his office playing chess by himself. "I find myself with the board and no one to play," he said, by way of greeting. "But it's more challenging this way." He lifted a knight and set it down with an audible click. "Checkmate," he said. He lifted his mug in a celebratory way. "I win again. Now what is it you want, Will?"

"I can't find any more baling twine for the furs. Who would I ask for it?"

Master George pushed back his chair and stretched out his legs on the desk. "It's cordage you need. It's yet another item not sent frequently enough from Home. Mind you, the stuff the locals make is at least as good. Just time-consuming to make, or so I'm told. Talk to – oh, God's blood, why don't I show you who to talk to."

He yawned and stretched and then dropped his feet to the floor. "It's particularly cold today; just the time to go outside and get soaked and miserable."

Master George was right. While the whistling wind and the cold inside the fort were difficult to endure, the wet, sharp wind was extremely unpleasant outside. With Master George wrapped in his furs and I in my white blanket, we pushed our way out of the doorway and down to a large building beside the main one. It was dark inside, and smelled strongly of curing furs.

Once inside we heard shouting and scuffling. Rounding a corner we entered the main hall. There was a group of men surrounding an Indian boy. He was bleeding from a ragged cut on his right side and his left hand was grasping his right bicep. There was blood seeping round his fingers.

"Sir!" shouted one skinny fellow. "We caught him having it out with Digger – Digger says he was sneaking around the stores – looking to steal some supplies, I'll bet." There was some jostling as the Indian prisoner was pushed one way and he pulled the other to try to free himself.

Master George walked over to the group. "Anything missing?" he asked.

"Not so's we've noticed as yet, but we haven't had much time to check," one man said.

"Where's Digger?"

"He's with the doc. This Indian got him good. Like he'll be lame for life."

Master George smoothed his chin and circled the group until he stood beside the Indian. "And you. What were you doing in the supply room? Who are you? You're not from around here."

The Indian turned full towards us, and I saw his face clearly for the first time. It was Kino Sesis, Amelia's cousin.

"Who do you know here? What were you trying to steal?" Master George prodded.

"No one. Nothing. I came to take back what was mine."

"We pay fair here. If you don't like the payment, you don't need to take it."

"It was not for trade. Your man took it. No payment."

"Are you alone?" Master George asked.

"Yes."

"Where are you headed?"

"South."

Master George was silent. Then he pointed to

one of the men. "Keep him until I have a chance to talk to Digger, see how injured he is." I made a sound and Master George turned. "What is it?"

"His arm," I said. "Shouldn't someone see to his arm?"

Master George turned back to the prisoner and looked him up and down, as if noticing the blood for the first time.

The man holding the Indian muttered, "The doc's busy. No time to fool with thieves anyway."

Master George nodded. "Yes, doc has been busy with some bloody mess or another. Do you know medicine, Will?"

"No –"

"Well, then –"

"But," I interrupted, "Amelia, you know, in the kitchen? She does."

There was more muttering among the men, but Master George nodded. "That she does. Take a message to her, Will, and tell her the man will be in the jailhouse. She can tend to him there as long as it doesn't interfere with her regular duties."

I left for the kitchen immediately, curious to know why this boy pretended not to know anyone, when it had been obvious that he knew not only Amelia but also at least some of the Home

Guard. What had Digger stolen? I had no doubts that the boy told the truth. I didn't expect Amelia to answer my questions. It wasn't really my business anyway. However, better to let her know what had happened and let her deal with it.

Finding Amelia crushing herbs with a pestle in the kitchen, I merely told her an Indian boy had been hurt and required treatment in the jail.

She set her work down immediately. "My cousin. Kino." She dusted off her hands and then asked, obviously hoping that she might be wrong, "It is the boy I spoke with yesterday?"

I nodded, and told her about his arm and his side.

She rolled her eyes and then went to get some of her herbal bags. Once she left the kitchen, I picked up the pestle and continued where she had left off. There was no longer much going on for most of the men, and eating was one of the few pleasures in an otherwise routine existence. If supper were late, we'd answer for it.

By the time she got back I had already begun serving the men. She had time only to say, "George is looking for you," before the din of plates and loud voices took over. I wiped my hands and then left the kitchen, being stopped and told messages to give to someone or another all the way to Master George's office.

"Cordage," he said, "the men have taken a bale up to the curing rooms for you. Tomorrow they'll show you how to prepare them."

"Thank you," I said. Master George waved a hand and went back to a book on his desk. I hesitated in the doorway, waiting for him to look up once more.

"Yes?" he said, finally, eyes still trained on a page.

"That boy…the one in the storeroom?"

"Yes."

"What was he doing in the fort?"

Master George looked up from his book, and leaned back in his chair.

"He was snooping around. They like to see how things are organized around here, I suspect. It's so different from what they're used to. Sometimes they want to see what we've got to exchange for furs. Perhaps they think we keep the best items hidden away somewhere. I don't know. Anyway, he's not going to be going anywhere soon."

"Why not?"

"The men got a little rough with him. Digger's got more friends than he knew, I think, although perhaps some just like a bit of a brawl to break up the monotony of days."

"So did he tell you why he was here?"

"No. He insisted Digger had stolen some important knife from him. Digger says he's never seen him before nor come across any valuables. Still, why pull a knife and hit Digger inside the fort? Unless he was startled at being caught out – unlikely, I'd say, since they usually have the reflexes of a cat and the hearing of a bat, and Digger isn't noted for his stalking abilities." Master George yawned and stretched. "Fortunately Digger just got a scratch on his calf; the men overreacted when they thought he had been hamstrung. Jittery. Ready for a fight." Master George shrugged. "Who knows? Another mystery for the London governors to ponder. They want records, and add rules for every contingency, even though by the time the pronouncements arrive the event is long past and forgotten. Nothing like having governors across an ocean directing us all."

He closed the book on his desk and said, "There will be other…incidents. Men and women are constantly coming and going here. Some won't leave soon enough for you. Things can heat up, and I don't mean the weather." He smiled, wryly. "I'm not saying any of the men are particularly dangerous, but it's less easy to keep an eye on everything come spring. In the winter, well, the men can go crazy cooped up here in this frozen prison. Things go missing. Fights occur. People get hurt. You're best to stick close to your duties and not wander too far off track."

I turned to go. I didn't bother mentioning that lately my duties had taken me out and around the fort more in one day than they had in my first month here. Unlike most of the employees of the fort, who had certain prescribed duties with little variation, I had slowly been given all the odds and ends jobs – running messages was an especially common one. I had gotten to know the men and their duties, and it had kept me from brooding on my life. But from what I had seen, I wasn't the only one who could benefit from a little variation to my days.

I returned to help Amelia with the bowls that were stacked high in the kitchen, but she wasn't washing them. Instead she was hurriedly stuffing things into a packsack. I greeted her and started pouring water from the iron kettle into the large sink.

"I'm going out for a time," Amelia said. "You can leave those bowls. I'll finish up when I get back."

"It's no trouble," I said. "How is your cousin doing?"

"Not good. The men beat him badly." Amelia

hesitated. "That one he injured – Digger – stole his sacred knife. It was very important that my cousin get it back. That weasel has taken many things from the Home Guard. It's just that up until now it has not been worth confronting him about it. They just watch him more carefully when he comes around. My cousin…did not know that."

"Did your cousin find it? Digger had it?"

Amelia smiled ruefully. "Yes. Kino's knife caused the other man's injuries." She wrapped her blanket tightly around her face and slipped a leather medallion through reinforced holes at the front to hold it in place. I moved closer to look at the pattern that was pressed into the leather. It was a darker imprint of a hare in midleap. It captured, in just a few arcs, the fleet-footedness, agility, and grace of the animal. Faint brush strokes at the ears and tail hinted at fur. The leather thong ended in intricate columns of quills dyed burgundy, blue, and white.

Amelia saw my stare and tapped the outline of the hare with her finger. "Working here I'm always jumping from one thing to another," she joked.

The next morning I awoke to unaccustomed silence. Usually at this time I could hear the muted sounds of Amelia pouring water, the sizzling sounds of goose cooking over the open fire, and the clatter of bowls as they were set out. I looked at the floor to see whether she had overslept, but she wasn't there. I rose, washed, and looked into the kitchen. The fire was still banked for the night, and almost out. Grey ash still outlined the shape of the logs that had been consumed by flame. Everything remained as it had been the night before. Where was Amelia? Why wasn't she back from wherever she had gone? I gnawed a fingernail, then went to fill the kettle with water and get a few things organized while I thought. Should I look for her? Tell Master George? Start the morning meal, and hope she returned soon? I hadn't ever had to prepare food for all the men by myself before, and, frankly, I did not care to try. I disliked the complaints and crabbiness whenever the tea was too weak or strong, the food too boring or bland, or conversely, too bitter. Amelia bore the brunt of it, of course, but I hadn't yet been able to accept it as graciously as she. I sometimes thought that no one worked harder than Amelia, and no one received less recognition of the fact. Well, I needed to do something. I decided to start the meal, and then inform Master George, who would wonder where

I was if I stayed to serve the whole meal. This decided, I set to with a will.

Despite my best efforts, the porridge had, I was repeatedly informed, a burnt flavour, the bread was doughy, and the tea, unsatisfactory. I tried to keep it simple, but I was so busy that by the time I saw Master George he had apparently already eaten. All I saw was his back as he left the kitchen to go to his office. I looked at the numbers of men still waiting to be fed and realized I would not be able to leave. Amelia was still not back. My worries increased. I worked as quickly as I could and finally the last man was seated and served. My aching back and sore arms attested that I had been at it for some time, but it seemed only moments before Master George was back in the kitchen, hands on hips, glaring at me.

"Where is Will?" he asked. Then, "Oh. It's you. Why aren't you at your post? Where is Amelia?"

"She's not here." I was thinking about how he had confused me with Amelia. Or had he just not looked? Amelia was taller than I and had long black hair whilst mine was brown. I guess people see what they expect to see.

Master George's voice was loud. "Well, where is she? She has no excuse to absent herself without permission. You are to be at work. I shouldn't have to come looking for you." He gestured at the bowls. "Leave those for her. If she's not going to complete her duties, then we'll find someone who will. Now come with me."

"She will. I mean, she's not well."

"She's ill?"

"She's unwell," I repeated. While I wasn't sure where she was, since she had intended to return before breakfast, something had gone wrong, which meant that something wasn't well. I hastily dried my hands. Master George was obviously upset about something. Surely not that Amelia wasn't there. I knew there was no one, other than myself as a very poor substitute, who could take over the cooking and cleaning and serving of all the men. They were too short-handed to dismiss anyone. People died in their jobs, after all.

"Send her to me once she recovers. That Indian boy has escaped. We need to ask her some questions about him. Perhaps she knows who he is or what he was doing here."

I followed him out of the kitchen and back to the trading room. I took the opportunity to ask Master George about some of the plants and berries I had seen and, as I had come to expect, he was not familiar with them. In London a Mr. Linnaeus was known for his knowledge of plants and their families. Perhaps Master George, I said, who had so many books in his office, might even have Linnaeus's work. He did – the famous two volumes entitled *Species Plantarum*, published in 1753. He also had useful studies of animals collected by others.

"If you do not find them there, then you may peruse some of these journals." Master George waved at full shelves of leather-bound books in his office. "We have had many scientists and explorers leave us copies of their works. You may read them in free moments, but you may not remove the books from this office. These are my only copies. But you might find something of interest in them." I expressed my appreciation, and then we set to work.

When we finished, it was midday, and I ran back to the kitchen to see if Amelia had returned. I dreaded the thought of having to prepare food for all the men again, but even more did I dread the thought of not seeing Amelia. That she might have gone away, perhaps forever, without saying goodbye, was constantly in my mind. However, the kitchen was almost warm and the kettles were steaming rapidly over the fire.

"You're safe!" I blurted out.

Amelia turned and smiled, but only briefly. "I

am sorry I was not back sooner. But bad things are stirring. I could not return last night. It is snowing hard, and it was too dangerous to travel." She shook her head. Her hair was unkempt, the plaits coming loose. I noticed that her eyes were red rimmed, and her face was drawn. Her hands were steady on their task, but her thoughts were obviously elsewhere.

"Master George wants to see you. He says your – that Indian boy – has escaped. He wonders if you know anything about it."

Amelia smoothed back her hair. "I will go see him after I serve the men."

"I can carry on here if you want to go now."

"You've done enough for me already. No, George will have to wait."

I heard no more about her cousin, his escape, or Master George's reaction until later. Soon there were other things to worry about and our conversations were short and frequently interrupted. It was three days before I even remembered, and then it was Digger himself who recalled it with a vengeance.

RUTTING MOON: OCTOBER, WHEN THE DEER ARE RUTTING

Digger sat in the kitchen yelling. Amelia had set a bowl of something in front of him, and as Master George and I went in the kitchen door we saw the whole bowl and all of its contents go flying. He had a large stick in his hand and was trying frantically to hit her with it. In one long stride, Master George was in front of me and seconds later beside the man.

"Digger, I see you are up and about! Not the best day for it with that foul wind blowing the fort to bits. How's the leg?"

Upon hearing Master George's voice, Digger struggled to stand, but Master George waved him down.

The man's face was flushed and his hair matted

and stiff with dirt. He lifted a trembling hand and wiped the spittle from his mouth. He eased himself back into his chair with a grunt. Then he said, "G'day, sir. The leg pains me still – but I'm going stark mad lying flat on my back day in and out."

Master George pulled out a chair and signalled to me to clean up the mess on the floor. I picked my way over to Amelia and took the cloth and water from her. I mopped up the mess while Master George and Digger talked.

"And this food! What *they* call food. I can't eat this slop."

Master George leaned back in his chair and I set his habitual water and rum in front of him. "No one can cook like Scotty could, that's certain. But no one else can cook like the girl does. We're managing. You just stay off that leg. Get him a tot, Will."

I took a mug from Amelia, who had done just that. The mug was full of rum. As I handed it to the man, he looked at me. The pained expression on his face was stark. I smelled his putrefying leg. It was swollen, and was obviously not healing. He drank his mug of rum neat and handed it back. Master George motioned to me to fill it again.

Digger wiped his mouth on his sleeve and sighed. "Ah, I was to go on the next ship. Now

I'll never make it back."

Master George said, "It's a long trip back, Digger. It would certainly pain your leg."

"I'll not last out the month. I'll be dead and buried in a week." He glared at Master George, as if daring him to deny it.

"The new medicine's not helping, then?"

Digger shook his head curtly.

"What does the doc – Dyer – say?"

"He wants to hack it off. My leg! I'll take my leg with me when I go. And she – that wench –" Digger gestured contemptuously at Amelia, "wants to put plant muck on it. Some kind of heathen remedy when the best of England's medicine can't help."

Master George nodded in agreement, though I thought trying anything surely couldn't hurt at this stage. Digger's face was now grey and drawn, and the smell of the leg was making me nauseated.

I hastily moved over to where Amelia was preparing the next meal, and, to take my mind off Digger, asked her about the healing plants.

She looked at me gratefully. "Purple coneplant would clean the wound and ease the leg. Dyer has left it too long, and he," she inclined her head ever so slightly towards Digger, "won't drink the medicinal tea I make him, nor allow me to exchange those dirty rags for a poultice on his leg."

"I don't think anyone could help him now. He's so angry," I said.

"No. He will die. His death could be eased, but he won't let me help. Still, he should be preparing himself for death, and he is not."

We watched Master George help Digger up from the table. Master George said in a soothing tone, "I'll find someone to read to you, Digger. Perhaps words from the Good Book would help."

"I ain't dead yet, sir."

"Of course not. But all the same, there's words worth reflecting on...." He nodded at me, and I went to get the Bible from his office. Although I knew much off by heart, I knew I would be more comfortable reciting with the book in my hands.

Whenever I looked at Digger, I was reminded of the stolen bag, but curiously, he never asked me about the proceeds, nor did he even seem to recognize me now. Perhaps being an apprentice of the Company and under Master George's eye gave me some small protection.

SEHKOS – WEASEL

One morning not long after Digger's tirade in the kitchen, Master George called me into his office. "We need a shroud made. There's been a death."

"Digger?"

Master George rubbed his forehead. "He died last night. Some are saying the knife was poisoned, that he died too quickly for it to be otherwise. If such is the case, then that Indian will be charged with murder."

"Murder?" I echoed. "But he was hurt as well; perhaps he was just defending himself."

Master George grunted and started for the door, saying, "I doubt it."

"Have they found the boy responsible?"

"Not yet. Come along. If anyone was defending himself, it was Digger, protecting the Company's property. No, if we find him or learn who he is, then he will answer for it. Digger may not have been the most amenable fellow, but he had his uses."

"When is the funeral?" I asked.

"Tomorrow before dark. Let's hope this infernal snow stops today. Fortunately, we don't have to find someone to chip at the frozen ground for a grave. Digger has dug extras. Never expected one to be for himself, I'm sure."

"He was out there a great deal. I always saw him there."

"Yes, now that you mention it, he did hang about there. Dismal place."

We reached the trade room and Master George showed me the fabric to be sewn into a shroud for Digger's body. Then we hiked from the fort to the burial grounds nearby to ensure there truly was a gravesite we could clear of recent snow, ice, and brush. Because the ground was frozen most of the year and there was little soil, Digger had gathered stones to add to the tops of the graves. We chose one spot and smoothed away a path for the pallbearers to take. It was while I was walking down to join Master George that I noticed something glinting in the weak midday sun. It came from one of the burial mounds. Before I could think better of it, I wandered over, curious to see what it could be. I walked around to the back and sucked in my breath. This was a burial mound, all right, but not of a body. I could see knives, a mirror, silver utensils, and even bits of glass. It was an obvious treasure trove, and someone had not replaced the rocks to properly cover the goods.

Master George was walking towards me. "What did you find? Not a man come back from the dead, is it?"

I pointed at the pile of goods. "I guess he hid some of his belongings here, safe from harm."

Master George whistled. "So Digger *was* hard at work up here – digging holes for treasure, though, not bodies!" He knelt down and rolled some larger stones away. "And look at this!" He carefully pulled out a long, slender object encased partially in fur and unwrapped it. It was a sword with a gilt handle and a leather scabbard. "And here we'd blamed the London boys." Master George brushed off some of the dirt that clung to the handle, and then looked at the heap of stones. "We'll have to replace them until there's time to dig it all up and decide what to do with it." His gaze fell on the sword. "We don't need the men seeing this."

We replaced and rearranged the rocks until everything was covered, except for the sword, which Master George slid through his belt under his huge buffalo robe. "It's starting to snow; let's go back. We'll deal with this later." We walked back towards the building and parted ways at the fort doors.

When I went in to the kitchen to warm myself, Amelia was speaking quietly to a young boy from the Home Guard. I watched him shake his head and mutter something over and over. Amelia handed him a package and then patted his shoulder. After a quick nod at me, he slipped out the door.

"Have they found your cousin?" I asked Amelia, rubbing my hands in front of the flames.

"No. More sickness. At a place not far from here. They were afraid it was the Pox."

"Small Pox? And is it?"

Amelia shuddered. "I think not. From his words, it is something else. Still bad, but not the Bad Death. There is no bad smell. The skin does not look burned. They do not feel on fire. But there are raised bumps on the arms and legs and they want to scratch."

"Could you help him? Was he from the sick family?"

"No. If there is any chance of Pox, then most no longer go near. Too many people die that way." She began putting her herbs away. "Having all die does no good." She pondered the steadily diminishing contents of her herbal bags. It had been a time of sickness. Her treatments had been much in demand. I too had been helped when I suffered from colds, aches, and other problems.

Amelia continued, "The sick family left a message and it was found by someone who told someone else. I gave that boy some salve to help with the scratching. Some syrup for the sore throat."

"A message written in your language? And how will he get the medicine to them?"

"No, not written. There are too many languages, even if we did write in letters, and many who pass by there may not know it. But a sign all could understand. I am the closest healer so he came to me. And the medicine will be given to the sick family the same way they gave others the sign. He will leave it at the same place." She started preparations for dinner, pulling out potatoes and onions and getting a knife to chop them up.

"Well, I'm glad it's not the Small Pox."

"As am I. We have lost too many from that

white man's disease. Too many elders, too many children. And to die in such a painful way. Families have killed themselves and their children when the signs have begun."

"Killed their children? How could they do that?" I was shocked.

"You have not seen us die of the disease," Amelia said grimly. "You white people die of it too, we know, but the blood does not burst from the body. You do not look as though you have been in the fire. You do not suffer in so much pain that you beg to be killed." Amelia shook her head.

"How have you seen this...and lived?"

"We have known this sickness in our family. Many many moons ago, long before my great-great-great-grandmother was born. We had this disease, and we have each had it in our lives – I as a small girl." Amelia chopped potatoes absently. "We did not all die. And now, our family is able, sometimes, to ease the death of one with the Pox."

I had been through plagues. I had lived. But the deaths were horrible and my attempts to ease suffering futile. Still, I had not considered, could not consider, ending their suffering any sooner though the plague-ridden had no hope of recovery. Had that been right? I shook my head. I lived now. My mother and brother had someone left to remember their lives and mourn their passing. I had done what I could.

Amelia smiled encouragingly at me. "Sit down. This illness is not the bad one. Do not worry. Now, where have you been? Did you have something to tell me?"

I told her about Digger's death. "Master George says if your cousin is found he will be charged with murder."

"Murder!" Amelia's eyes flashed. "Yes, I was told he was dead. And no thought given to his own actions. Or that he died from ignorance, not murder."

"Some men think the knife was poisoned."

Amelia laid her knife on the counter and reached for a large iron pot. She was silent for a moment and then she said quietly, "That is not true. My cousin was cut with the same blade, and he lives. That man was unclean and he did not eat well. But my cousin is far away now, safe from all their thoughts."

"I am glad," I said.

Amelia handed me the pot filled with potatoes to hang on the fire. "I want you to hear me. It's *that* one. The one you call Dyer. He is looking for something. Weasel – Digger – has been unable to run jobs for Dyer and will not be running anymore for him now. Dyer is restless. Keep out of his path."

I shuddered. "Thanks for the warning. I have an uneasy feeling when I see him."

"Yes, uneasy is a good way to feel." Amelia looked approvingly at me. "He is clever, though his so-called medicine punishes more than it heals. Weasel was not, and we saw his thoughts. Now bad things are happening, and sometimes the pattern is not clear."

"Like what bad things?"

"Dyer brings sickness. Trouble. Death."

"Trouble I can see. But sickness? How? Is his medical training that poor?"

Amelia shook her head in disgust. "You don't want to see what he does. Causing pain is his main practice. When he stops his work, the sick one briefly feels better, if you could call that helpful. Still, if one gets away from him short an ear or a nose, one could count oneself lucky, especially if Dyer has been drinking."

I felt sick myself. "He really is bad, then."

Amelia agreed. "As for the trouble he causes, we are not yet sure of his misdeeds. But where he walks, bad things follow."

Master George appeared in the doorway with brown burlap sacks draped over one arm. "Will – oh, Amelia." Master George looked stern. "I want to see you when we get back. Will, let's take care of that inventory business."

"I'll get my blanket," I said. Amelia was teaching me how to sew a fur coat for winter, but it was slow work. Master George followed me to the door and shifted the burlap to another arm. He held out two books. "I came across some spare journals in the storeroom," he said. "Since you have expressed an interest, I thought you might like to sketch some of those plants and animals you've seen."

I gave him my thanks as I took them from him, for I had seen many specimens that I could find no record of in the books from England. Others were mentioned in explorers' journals that Master George kept copies of, but nowhere had I found all the plants and birds that I saw with Amelia. I was very pleased to see the thick creamy paper and ruffled edges contained therein.

"I will try to put them to good use," I said, smiling.

"You are pleased, then," Master George said, smiling in return. "I'm glad. Put them away for now and let's take care of that chore."

I hastily put the books on the sill and followed Master George outside.

Master George motioned to me to walk alongside him. "We'll be able to fill sacks while the men eat. Less chance someone will see us then," he said, by way of explanation.

"With all the treasure Digger had hidden," I said to Master George as we walked, "could it be possible, do you think, that he *did* take that boy's knife?"

Master George looked at me in surprise. "Eh? You are protective about that boy, aren't you? Not a distant relative, or anything, is he?" He walked a moment in silence, pondering, before he said, "It's possible, I suppose. Nothing was taken from the Company stores and, as you point out, Digger always did have a penchant for, shall we say, collecting things. I hadn't realized quite the extent of his predilection, I must admit."

As we turned the corner and began the short walk to the graveyard, two boatmen appeared, nodded to Master George, and fell into step behind us. Once we were at the site, Master George directed us to carefully remove all rocks and snow. Strong winds had blown the new snow into hard, crusted drifts. The men used hatchets to hack the snow into blocks and then we lifted them out. Then we began filling coarse brown sacks with all manner of things, although none as valuable as the golden sword Master George had already removed. The two boatmen then slung the bags on their backs and left in the direction of the boathouse.

While pushing aside gravel and snow, I caught a glimpse of rope, and managed to pull it out. It was my bag from England. It was empty. I looked around for my belongings, but could find nothing.

"That's sufficient," Master George hissed. "Now let's fill in the holes – get rid of our footprints and digging marks." He handed me a shovel and I used the back to smooth the area as quickly as I could. The two boatmen returned and helped me, then we walked back to the fort. It was dark, and very cold. I hurried to my room near the kitchen to wash and warm myself, then entered the kitchen to inform Amelia that Master George was ready to see her.

"Well, I do have to see him about my leaving the fort. This might as well be the time."

The next morning when I met with Master George, he was looking at the staffing lists and the names of those who, while not officially on the payroll, performed many useful services for the Company.

With Digger dead, and my position somewhat more secure, I broached the subject of the stolen goods in a roundabout way. "Amelia has provided me with clothing of her own because I had nothing suitable. She is helping me sew a winter coat and moccasins, among other things. I would like to transfer some of my pay –"

Master George laughed. "The thought of money is wearing a hole in your pocket?"

"No, of course not. But I do want to offer her recompense for her kindness."

Master George rose from his desk and poured himself a drink from a flask he kept behind some books. He took a long swallow and said, "That sounds reasonable. Why don't you send her to me and we'll settle the accounts."

"Thank you. Also...." I watched Master George pour himself another small amount from the flask. He turned to look at me when I hesitated.

"Go on, lass. We don't have all day. To whom else do you owe 'recompense'?"

"To Digger, sir. At least, that's whose goods I traded when I arrived –"

"Was Digger aware that you were trading his goods?" Master George sat down at his desk with a thump. He was looking at me with narrowed eyes, likely having second thoughts about having offered me a contract with the Company.

"Yes, I met him...he sent me in...I'm not sure..."

Master George sighed patiently. "So Digger met up with you somehow, gave you his goods and sent you in to trade them. You didn't give him those tokens, is that it?"

"No, that's not it. I mean, yes, I gave him the tokens but the goods...I'm not sure if the trade goods were his...."

Master George laughed. "Oh, is that all? Truly? Well, lass, if they weren't his, and no one has come forward to complain, then the secret of whose they were has gone to the grave with Digger. Just as well. That man had a number of secrets that are best left undisturbed. Now let's get to work on these staffing lists."

Because I was often with Amelia when I wasn't with Master George, he had come to learn of the many things she accomplished. He was astonished to learn that Miki Siw was her brother. "But I thought Amelia was from the Home Guard! They come and go from this area, you know, so I had assumed she had not been back for some years. So that's why I didn't recognize her. I had no idea she wasn't from here."

I don't expect he ever really thought before

about who had repaired or made certain things. Like the stuffs from England, it mattered not to him who had made them, just that they were at hand when required. Master George told me that he had forgotten Amelia would be leaving and that another would arrive to replace her. Still, he said he was relieved he wouldn't have to split my duties with cookery chores. The new cook was a young girl, called Siki, Amelia had told him, who was unused to fort life. Perhaps I could help her to adjust, being relatively new here myself, Master George suggested.

SÎKISOWIN – FEAR

Sîkisowin arrived a few days later. I think we were all taken aback. She was tiny, and followed Amelia around like a miniature shadow. A shout, a door slamming, an order would startle her. She had been given her own place in our small room, but it was not one night before she moved her furs over to Amelia's and slept beside her instead. Amelia, who until then had been growing more and more excited about leaving the fort, counting the days and nights and sewing something almost every night and before dawn each morning, suddenly became subdued.

"It will not work, Willa," Amelia said one night, when Siki, as we called her, had finally been convinced to take a message to Master George. "How my people could agree to send one so young to a place like this! They know what it is like here! She is not safe to stay!"

"But she says she is more than your eighteen years," I reminded Amelia.

"Perhaps in seasons," Amelia replied, "but in no other way. When I think about leaving her here alone...."

"She's doing fine," I soothed. "She just needs to get used to the place."

"I must find out why they sent her. There must be someone more experienced."

Unlike Amelia, who spoke the English tongue more fluently than some of the Company's employees, Siki's words in English were hard to understand. She had trouble with certain sounds and meanings too. I had noticed that the Home Guard also had this difficulty, but that Amelia and her brother, Miki Siw, did not. When I asked Amelia why this was, she told me that her ancestors had always travelled far, learned many languages and customs of others, and then passed their teachings on to their children. "We journey and we speak with others in their own tongue to prevent misunderstanding. We trade what we have learned with others. My people are few, but we have been fortunate. Others are not so lucky. Siki comes from a different clan. She was not taught other tongues from the time her eyes peeped open. And you know," Amelia shrugged, "once one is grown it is hard to learn and speak other tongues, *n'est-ce pas?*"

Siki did not want to speak in English. She did not like to have her words or the pronunciation corrected, even when Amelia would remind her that she was to teach the rest of her clan when she returned home.

"It's better *we* know what you say about us, than what you *tell* us you say," Amelia said to me by way of explanation, when once again she refused to answer Siki in her own language. Siki missed her home and her friends and her family. And ever so quietly, she began to resent Amelia's insistence on speaking and learning English ways and work. And because I was an English person, she began to resent me. The tension between us grew. And so, partly, I think, to mollify Siki, Amelia continued teaching me new words, but also began teaching me words in her own and Siki's tongues – for they both spoke different languages. Siki would listen to my painful attempts to get my mouth around the long, complicated words that were so easy for her to know and say.

Only then did her demeanour become more cheerful. She began to speak English words and patiently began to help me with words that, I knew, babes in their cradles could utter with ease. And so we became friends.

One night soon after Siki came, a vicious storm struck. After a clear, still evening came winds so harsh and biting that we woke to an inch of frost on our blankets, the walls, the floor. Amelia was up first, as usual, and had draped a blanket over the parchment that covered the window in our small room. It moved stiffly in the whistling wind. Eventually we located a second piece of parchment to place over the first, though the cold and wind still blew through to us. We remained cold for many months.

FROST MOON: NOVEMBER, WHEN THE RIVERS FREEZE OVER

Sometimes I went with Amelia to see the Home Guard people, or others who lived within the fort walls. And finally it occurred to me what puzzled me. Amelia seemed entirely different when we were alone with her people, especially when we were outside York Factory. For one thing, I could see her face. She stood tall and straight when we walked, and inside a lodge the leather thong held the blanket around her shoulders instead of covering her hair and face. Her voice rang out strong and clear; she smiled. In the summer and autumn, I remembered how she had looked around her with great interest, her eyes caught by snow geese and ducks flying overhead, by cries and shouts from others. She always walked in long strides so that I had to run to keep up. But back in York Factory she changed. As if a shabby grey netting was flung over her, or the weight of twenty years, her back and shoulders were hunched, her head and hair covered by a blanket, her face always down, her hands busy with work, her words whispered, her movements stiff and contained.

One night, when the sky was clear and the moon shone bright and we couldn't sleep for cold, I teased her that there seemed to be two Amelias, the one who worked in York Factory and was old and stiff, and the one I saw with the Home Guard, who was strong and happy and filled with fun.

"Do you not feel different when you leave the fort?" Amelia asked curiously.

"I feel small. I feel scared that I might get lost."

"How odd! When I am away from this place, I feel big! I feel as if I have come back to life. Inside here, I put on a self that is too small and I cannot stand up straight or move properly. The longer I am here, the smaller that self gets. I must keep getting smaller in order to fit back inside this small self. And I keep my face down because there is nothing for my eyes to see. That self is not me."

"But why isn't it you?" I asked. "I think I'm the

same person I was when I left England. I'm in a different place, but I'm still the same."

Amelia didn't answer immediately. She sat up from her spot on the floor and pulled out the quillwork that she worked on whenever she had a free moment.

"It is becoming me," she said finally. "Which is why I must leave here soon. I feel myself becoming smaller and smaller, and soon when I look at myself I will not be there."

"What do you mean?"

"In this place, all men see is a blanket with legs. Once that was good. It meant I could do my work without trouble. Now it is bad. If you act like something else for long enough, then you could become something else. I am afraid I am becoming something else. Or perhaps I have always been just a blanket with legs. Perhaps I have never been as I see myself."

I rolled off my elbow and sat up. "No. You are different when we are outside. Everyone there sees you as you really are. But I think I know what you mean. In here, no one sees me, either. But then, no one has ever seen me. I'm invisible." I tried to laugh, as if it were a joke. But Amelia didn't join in.

"I see you, Willa," she said simply.

SHORT DAY MOON: DECEMBER, WHEN DAYS ARE SHORT AND NIGHTS LONG

The bitter, dark cold stayed for long, barely endurable months. The sun disappeared for longer and longer periods. Our movements were so severely restricted because of the unbearable cold, storms, and blizzarding gales that it became urgent to find something – anything – to do. The men played cards, drank, and fought. Or they would lie motionless, staring into space, until the cold forced them to move about.

The fires burned always. But a kettle of water could freeze only a foot from the flame. Often our eyes burned from the smoky rooms. The days dawned grey and then turned black. Weeks and months passed with little sunlight, and I think its prolonged absence affected all our spirits. Grey sky seemed to meet frozen ground in one seamless monochrome.

We lit the lamps upon rising in the dark, and their acrid, smoky, oily film coated us and the walls in a sooty ash. Ice, inches thick, covered the inside walls. The air was dry and the weight of the clouds oppressive. Amelia was the only one who seemed unaffected in word or deed. She was constantly busy helping injured people who were brought to York Factory or who came from the Home Guard. Starving men, women, and children from the territory outside the fort would come for food and warmth. The sick and elderly, especially after a spell of particularly harsh weather, would come to the Home Guard Indians who would then notify Amelia. The men of the fort often went first to Dyer when ill, but many also came secretly to Amelia.

She and Siki were also busy cooking meals, making and repairing hundreds of tall moccasins, leggings, tunics, and snowshoes. I gave what small help I could. I could cut out the leather and do some repair work, but any patterns or proper stitching – to make a tightly sealed moccasin, for instance – was difficult for me. The snowshoes were huge, as tall as the one who was to wear them. Amelia showed me how to make them, although she always needed to fix the final details herself. However, my frustration would melt away when Amelia began one of her marvellous tales while we worked. We laughed and talked and toiled, and sometimes I would be so engrossed that an interruption would shake me from a world of warmth and colour and laughter back to one of frosty walls and frigid air, a world of starkness.

Amelia would often ask me about my life after a story about hers, but my life seemed thin and circumscribed by comparison. I also could not draw conclusions and express opinions as she could. I seemed to have so little experience on which to draw. The house she had grown up in appeared to be the whole wide world, while mine had been restricted to one small room – with a closed door. Still, though much of our lives had been different, there were also common threads, and we laughed when we came across these too; laughter in the solitary stillness, where no birds sang for months on end.

We began to see Dyer more frequently near the places where we worked and walked. The first time he came upon the three of us, he quickly took Siki's small hand in both of his and bent over her in a chivalrous fashion. Siki, who had begun to feel more comfortable upon finding that she was quite unnoticed, trembled like a mouse near the claws of a cat. Amelia reluctantly introduced the two, but said only that Siki was there to assist her. But Dyer already knew Amelia was to leave soon. Whenever we took Siki around afterwards, we could not seem to avoid him.

He restricted himself to brief courtesies when I alone crossed his path, but when I was with Amelia, he would often request personal services from her – a favourite one was to barber him. "Even my surgical knives aren't as sharp as yours, Amelia. No one can give me as close a shave as you," he would assure her. Since she performed many essential duties at the fort, not least cooking, laying up food stocks, and making and repairing clothing and travelling gear, I thought his little requests were designed to discomfit her, since I found it quite apparent that she disliked the man, but perhaps I was wrong about that and he really did not know. Still, we looked very carefully for him when we went outside alone.

Unlike many of the men, Dyer was often washed and combed. He had someone to look after his clothes, because they were always clean and mended. Burgundy and black were his favourite colours, and he frequently asked Amelia to supply someone with plant dyes for his scarves, sashes, and hat ties. When I commented on the red colour, Amelia responded bitingly, "It's because of all the bloodletting he does; you can't have a cold around Dyer without him wanting to wield a knife!"

When he volunteered to show Siki around, I thought Amelia would show her anger, but her refusal was mild enough. His words to Siki were so gracious, however, that she actually smiled at him, a rare event. After that, Amelia quickly marched us back to the kitchen where she gave Siki another lecture on the men in the fort and about Dyer in particular.

"But he seems nice," Siki protested at one point. Amelia looked incredulously at me, then turned back to Siki.

"He is a butcher! And a murderer! The Home Guard say he beat a girl – to death – because she would not go with him."

I was shocked. "Was that the trouble he had back home in London? Why he came here?"

Amelia frowned. "No, this was not far from here. He was sent away to a different fort for a time, in the hopes that her family would not find him."

I shook my head. "I know the trouble was

something serious – I believe he was charged and he came to Hudson's Bay to avoid any punishment."

"Well, this happened here. Before I came. He was sent away to a different fort for his own safety. His safety!" Amelia said. "He is a rattlesnake," Amelia jabbed her fingers in an evil eye sign. "He will strike if you step too close."

"That would not happen to us," Siki said proudly. "How could he possibly harm us?"

"Tell her what befell you," Amelia directed me. I did, and Siki seemed subdued after that. From then on, when we came across Dyer, Siki stood with her eyes, even her head, facing down. Try as he might to gain her attention, Siki would not look at him. Amelia did, however, and Dyer's smiles at her were chilling.

COLD MOON: JANUARY, WHEN THE SEVERE COLD SETS IN

We could not be with Siki forever, though. We each had work to do. One afternoon I entered the kitchen quietly and stopped abruptly. Dyer was there, standing over Siki, who was leaning away from him. Her blanket had slipped down over her shoulders, and Dyer was sliding his hand up and down one of her shining black plaits. Siki's face was turned away from him, and the knuckles on the one hand I could see were white as they gripped a table behind her.

"Siki!" I said, but my voice was not loud. Still, Dyer let go of her plait and turned to look at me.

"Siki," I said again. "Master George wants to see us. Right away."

"Yes, please," Siki said. But Dyer didn't move. Siki timidly pushed one of his arms out of the way and squeezed past. As soon as she was near me, I took her arm and we walked quickly out of the kitchen. I didn't dare look back. I stole a quick look at Siki's face. Had I done the right thing? Then she looked at me. Her face was strained. "I'm glad it was you. Amelia would be so mad."

I stopped as we neared Master George's office. "Master George doesn't really want to see us now," I confessed. "It was just the first thing that came to mind when I saw Dyer."

Siki stopped as well. "I understand," she said calmly, and surprisingly, she smiled, fingering a brightly beaded necklace I hadn't seen before that hung around her neck. "Thank you." She turned softly and disappeared down the walkway.

Master George's door was open and I looked in. He was writing something, seeming very absorbed. I started to tiptoe away when he caught sight of me and called me in.

"Listen to this, Will." He cleared his throat and began to read from the paper in front of him.

The bright sun was extinguished, and the stars
Did wander darkling in the eternal space,
Rayless, and pathless, and the icy Earth

Swung blind and blackening in the moonless
air;
Morn came and went – and came, and brought
no day,
And men forgot their passions in the dread
Of this their desolation; and all hearts
Were chilled into a selfish prayer for light.

His voice trailed off, and he stared grimly at the papers before him.

"It's very descriptive," I said, although in truth I felt disheartened. "I'm not sure it would encourage visitors, however."

Master George had already picked up his quill to continue his work when my words penetrated.

"Eh, Will?" He set down his quill and looked at me. "Are you making a joke? I think you are! I believe that is the first one I've heard from you." He smiled at me.

I smiled back, thinking about the many jokes Amelia and I shared as cheer in this dark place.

Master George continued to look at me. "Just what is your real name, Will? I don't believe you have ever told me. Nor where, exactly, your family is from."

Surprised by his sudden interest, I said, "My name is Willa, close enough to Will to be serviceable. My family's estate was near Southampton, though it is gone, now. Our family name is Thompson."

"What, is your father old Joseph Thompson? Why, he had a distinguished career with the Hudson's Bay Company."

"No, sir, he is my great-uncle. My father is dead. My entire family is gone, in fact, other than he."

"But old Thompson had a good many pounds salted away. He's not run through them so soon?"

"No, sir. He is still a wealthy man."

"Then I don't understand what he was about," George said, "sending you on the supply ship to York Factory. What on earth was he thinking?"

"I don't know, sir. My brother, Charles, had planned to come to York, but he died before making the journey."

George shook his head wonderingly. "What kind of future did he think you might have? And how did he get you on a ship? He must have given a weighty bribe!"

"My great-uncle was quite keen to have me leave London."

"I imagine he must have been. But to what intent? I cannot fathom it! You had no experience living or working here as an Indian lass would…just think what might have become of you!"

"I was worried about that, but it's worked out well, fortunately."

"Life does go on, I suppose, and you seem to be making the best of it. You must be what age now, twelve, thirteen?"

"Almost sixteen, sir."

"Is that right?" Master George looked astonished and was uncharacteristically silent for a moment before musing aloud, "A young English lady in our midst. That is a novelty, now. Has no lonely bachelor asked for your hand? Not one?"

"No, sir, unless you count the jesting of the traders when I first arrived."

"Remarkable. York isn't exactly teeming with eligible young ladies. You're quick, accomplished in many regards…." Master George fell silent once more, regarding me. Finally he said abruptly, "Well, I must finish this." He gestured expansively at his papers, dismissing me.

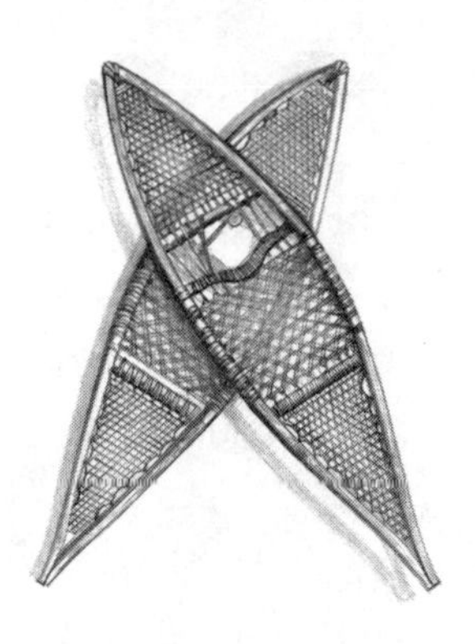

OLD MOON: FEBRUARY, WHEN THE WINTER IS OLD AND THE DAYS GROW LONGER

When the days finally began to hold cold sunlight, Master George and the senior men planned a party. Master George assured me that this party would not be the free-for-all that others had been. This party was for those left holding the fort – a winter's-end party. Even an important official and his wife would attend this one, coming by dogsleigh and snowshoe from another fort on the Hudson's Bay. The recovered sword was to be presented to the man that night in a ceremony. Master George went on and on about what I needed to do. Since in the last few months he had been content to have me carry out my duties with just the sketchiest of instructions, I was quite surprised at his concern over every detail.

Finally I said, "Is there something else you're concerned about? I think we've looked after everything."

Master George, for once, seemed at a loss for words. He leaned back in his chair and folded his arms. Then, looking away from me, he muttered a few words.

"Pardon me?"

"Perhaps – perhaps you could plan on attending," Master George said.

Visions of parties past replayed themselves in my head. Drunken brawls, blood, emergencies, shouts, and gunshots. Often impromptu, spilling out from the kitchen to the hall to outside. For some, Amelia said, the entire visit to the fort was a party – a reprieve from the arduous work trapping and hauling furs, traversing the land and water – a reprieve from the hazards of winter. Amelia, I, and some others had often gone to pick herbs and berries when the revelry became entirely out of hand. Fortunately, since I had arrived near the end of the summer season, I had missed many of them.

"Really, it will be nothing like the other parties," Master George said hastily. "This one will be quite civilized. There will be dancing and singing, dinner of course, conversation.... You will enjoy yourself, I'm sure. A reward of sorts for your work to date."

I hesitated. Dancing? Singing? And Master George inviting me? I felt nervous at the prospect; but on the other hand, perhaps this was some sort of order. How could I refuse?

"It's not an order," Master George said, as he waited for my answer.

"Well," I said, thinking about who would be there. Dyer, for one.

"Why don't you come? Bring Amelia. She's leaving soon; bring that little replacement of hers as well. We have two manservants arriving to cook and to serve our guests, and so your friends would not be required in that regard."

I couldn't imagine either one wanting to go, but I would ask. "Perhaps. I'll see."

"Good, good!" Master George beamed, inordinately pleased, I thought.

When I told Amelia and Siki, Amelia shook her head. "No," she said. "I am leaving soon. I will not go." Siki, surprisingly, was very excited.

"Our people will not be there this time," Amelia reminded her. "There will be all those white men." She appealed to me. "She has no idea what it will be like."

I agreed. I had begun to feel obliged to attend,

however, and I truly hoped they would come with me. "Master George says it will be different. An official and his wife will be there. There won't be so many attending. There won't be as much drinking."

"Did George say we must be present?"

"He invited you both as guests, not in any serving capacity."

"Had you told him you would attend?"

"No, but if you will go then I will also. I think I must."

"Ah." Amelia looked at me slyly. "Of course. Well then, Siki, to please George we will all go."

I laughed. "What do you mean?"

Amelia laughed too and said, "You will see."

Siki looked back and forth between us, puzzled, but her thin small face lit up at the thought of a celebration.

I helped Master George make sure all the trading goods were locked up tight. Nothing was to be left out or accessible. Not that anyone attending the party would make off with anything, Master George told me; but those who didn't go might take the opportunity to help themselves. I helped Amelia ensure we had all the necessary supplies ready for the substitute cooks, and then we arranged tables and chairs in a room we rarely saw

– the officers' meeting room. Siki made some beautiful dried flower arrangements for the tables. It made the room look quite festive.

The day of the party was a rarity. The sky was clear, the winds were calm, the air still. Amelia, Siki, and I planned our finery – very different from dress standards of parties past in my old home, but certainly more appropriate than satin and gauze.

Later, while I sat cleaning my moccasins in preparation for the evening, Amelia came over to me. She held out a garment worked entirely in quills.

"This was to be my farewell gift to you, but I thought tonight you might like to wear it."

I took it from her and unfolded it. It was a vest, made from fine white deerskin, soft and supple. The outside was quilled in white, with hues of burgundy, green, and gold. "It's a white willow," Amelia said, taking it from me and showing me the back. "Here are its roots, anchored near water." She traced the slender white branches as they rose from the bottom of the vest. The bottom was dark blue, then green, then pale blue, then white. "And here are your friends, watching over you," Amelia said, smiling. She pointed to a full moon quilled on the back. "My mother, the moon. And here," she pointed to an eagle, "my brother, Miki Siw." She pointed to a black bear below. "My father." I nodded my understanding. "But where are you?" I asked.

"Don't you see me?" Amelia asked me seriously.

I took the vest carefully from her hands and looked closely. I knew her sign was the hare, but I could see no hare. I looked at the trim of the vest, I looked on the inside leather, I looked at each colour on the vest, but I could see no hare. I rubbed my eyes and the vest, slippery and heavy, began to slide off my knees. I grabbed it quickly and spread it out once again, upside down this time, on my lap, and there she was. The outline of a hare, in sketches of colour, touched every corner of the back of the vest, encompassing the whole yet leaving each entity intact. I looked up and met Amelia's eyes.

"I will be with you even when you cannot see me," Amelia said quietly. "You are my sister."

)) ● ((

That evening I could almost believe without too much effort that I was at some unusual party back in England. There was all that Master George had said, and suddenly it seemed so familiar: the music, the carefully orchestrated dancing, the polite conversation. It wasn't until late in the evening that something occurred to mar the occasion. I had just returned to our table after another dance with Master George when Dyer came to ask Amelia to dance – and she too quickly refused. She said she did not dance, but Dyer was not pleased. After a long moment, it was to Siki that Dyer turned and she, seemingly flattered, shyly danced the night away.

The official's wife, after expressing her amazement that a white woman would dare work in such a place unprotected, had many questions for me, as did I about her own experiences. We reminisced about many things from home and studiously avoided discussing anything unpleasant. She was anxious to return to England to collect her son, who had been sent to study there, while I, to my own surprise, had no such desire to return. But for a few hours I slipped back into something like my old life and time passed very quickly.

It was that night that Master George asked me to marry him. He filled my astonished silence with reasons why such a marriage would be advantageous for me. "You'll be well looked after, of course. I am young, in good health, and of a marrying age. My future is stable here, so you needn't worry about financial security. While I like the occasional drink, I don't drink to excess, nor beat others, man or woman. You needn't fear me. I would treat you well." He had obviously given it much thought.

However, it was equally apparent to both of us that I had no such inclination. I was surprised at that, and I think George was a bit as well. Why was I not thrilled, or at least grateful for the offer? Here in the wilds I would have protection and secure circumstances – far more than I had had since my straitened family circumstances had begun. But my new life here was a whole new world to me. I had, almost without realizing it, come to appreciate the knowledge that I was supporting myself and learning a trade. For the first time in my life, I had freedom to make a certain number of decisions – minor though they might be. By marrying, I would be giving this all away, wouldn't I?

After a too long, awkward silence, Master George asked quietly, "Do you intend to marry someone else?"

I shook my head without a word.

He persisted, "Do you intend to fulfill your contract, then?"

I thought about it for a moment. I was determined not to marry. At least, not yet. I wanted, however, to continue working. I had grown accustomed to thinking of my five-year obligation to the Company. I had not considered doing anything else since signing the contract. I told Master George this.

He sat with his head bowed for some moments. He spoke, finally. "You are young, yet. All of this," he waved his arm around, "is still new to you. I can understand that. Nevertheless, please think about it and let me know if you change your mind."

I stood when he did and waited uncertainly.

He smiled, painfully it seemed to me. "Don't worry. This will change nothing between us."

Still, the next few weeks were uncomfortable ones. Master George began to avoid me, sending me orders through others and making our conversations brief when we met. However, it was impossible for him to avoid me entirely. I think that is why Master George eventually called me into his office with another proposal, a business one this time. He had received notice through a mail packet that the new fort on the Kisiskachiwun River was desperately in need of a clerk. While Master George now expected a new apprentice on the next supply ship, it was obvious to him that a new recruit, unused to life in this place, would be of little immediate use. He also expected the Factor's return on the next supply ship, and he was concerned for my future if I remained here, unmarried, and working for the Company. It might produce some sort of scandal if news got back. He proposed, therefore, sending me – me! – to the wilds where few English ventured, where great woolly beasts and vast prairie fires raged and killed. Sending me to places that had driven men mad with fear and hunger and loss. He would hire some people to take me there and provision the group with the necessary supplies. I would be perfectly safe, he said. And it would be a temporary assignment. A year, perhaps two.

He waited for a response. I nodded stiffly – afraid to speak. I thought of how my great-uncle had, without a word to me, secretly planned to change my circumstances entirely. Now Master George was doing the same. At least, I thought, Master George told me in advance of shipping me off.

Master George said, finally, "I will begin arrangements, then."

I nodded once more before stumbling my way out of his office and back to the kitchens, where Amelia, upon seeing me, fixed a hot tisane and sat me down on the bed in our sleeping quarters. I managed to stutter out what Master George had said. Her reaction, however, was not one of sympathy. She clapped her hands and laughed.

"You lucky girl, you! You will leave this place of death too! I am so happy for you!" She jumped up and immediately began to plan. "You will leave at Egg Moon, of course. And on the Kisiska-chiwun River! There are very fine places to stop along the way! Oh, you will love one place – it is my favourite place in the grasslands...." she stopped suddenly. "But what is it? Why do you sit bent over as if you have been dealt a death blow? By the Great Mother, what is the matter?"

The hot drink seemed to brace me, and I could suddenly speak. I told her I feared I was being banished – given a term of exile in some wild prison. I poured out all my fears and disappointments to her. I told her also about refusing Master George's other offer.

She sat down beside me and put her arm around my shoulders. "You are young yet," she said gently, echoing Master George's words. "You have seen little of the world. You have much to learn. You have told me so yourself," she reminded me. I nodded miserably.

"You will go to a place where there are few white men...." Amelia stopped, obviously realizing that this might not be the comfort to me that it was to her. "It is warmer there. There is lots of game, lots of food. Many flowers and blue skies, not like this cloud-filled ice bog. The rivers flow swift and clear. In the warm season, the colours in the skies are red and yellow and pink. There are many spiritual places. The people...oh, there are so many friends who live around there. My father is often there." She looked at me consideringly. "My mother and brother too. Soon I also will pass through."

I looked up at her. "You might too? Do you really think so?"

Amelia smiled. "I am leaving here, too, remember?" She jumped up again, excited. "It is possible that...." she stopped. "Well, I must check into something. George can be a good man, can't he? Perhaps in a few years, after you have seen more of the English men here, you will change your mind about him. He is not so bad, you know. Now I must plan. But please do not be sad. This is wonderful news." There was a knock on our door, and Amelia was asked to minister to a woman in childbirth. I followed Amelia into the kitchen, where she swiftly selected dried herbs and then rushed away.

Master George, a good man? And Amelia happy for me? I rubbed my forehead, feeling suddenly tired. Perhaps I should consider this more carefully. I knew Amelia was happy for me and I knew why, but Master George? Was he not attempting to rid himself of me? I believed he approved of my work and seemed to favour my person. Was he sending me away because he valued my work, perchance? So that I could learn more of the business and be of some useful assistance to the men of the new fort? Perhaps it was a combination of factors, for I could not deny that he now felt awkward in my presence. Still, he was not shipping me to London where I had no hope of opportunity, but instead transferring me to another place. For a year or two, he had said, which meant he expected, possibly even hoped, to see me again.

I was afraid to leave York Factory, however. Master George had told me of his hideous trials in the wilderness, and I had heard many other Company men's tales of misadventure. Master George had been thankful to return to York; though even here, at the oldest English fort, he said, the semblance to civilization was faint.

I finished my hot drink and set the mug on the sill. I took a deep breath. At worst, I would be killed during my own proposed journey. Frankly, I had expected that to happen many times since leaving England – almost hoping during some particularly miserable moments.

"What are you afraid of, then?" I heard my brother, Charles, say in my mind. "Embrace this chance to see the New World!" I could see his eager face before me, ready to launch into a discourse on the wonders of exploration. I had to smile, thinking of him. I knew so well what he would say to me. He himself would have leapt at the opportunity.

I retied the bags of herbs Amelia had left out and put them away. Slowly I felt my spirits rise. Perhaps it wouldn't be so terrible. I tried not to think of all the perils just yet. About the wild animals. The forests. The lack of four walls and of my vulnerable thin skin. Like Amelia, I too would plan. I would begin by looking over Master George's maps. Where was I going? How far away was this new fort? By focusing my attention on obtaining information, perhaps I could quell my fears about all that I did not know. I heard Charles cheer at my efforts to change my heart. I knew that, if he were alive, he would be pleased with me.

EAGLE MOON: MARCH, WHEN THE EAGLES APPEAR

Planning my travels meant a great many discussions and filled many hours when I was with Master George. Our getting married was not mentioned again. There were, however, numerous things to work out about my trip to the new fort – not least when and with whom I would leave. Master George wanted to ensure my safety as much as he could on such an arduous journey and he considered and then rejected many offers to take me there. The days passed and these two questions remained unanswered.

Then one afternoon I came upon him and Amelia in the kitchen; they both turned with broad smiles at my greeting. "We have someone to take you, Will!" Master George announced. "Amelia's family will be going in that direction – you couldn't find a better guide. I met Amelia's mother when I travelled out one year. A remarkable woman. Most remarkable."

He paused and Amelia spoke up. "I did not want to tell you until I was sure it could be arranged."

I was surprised. "But how did you ask her? I thought you hadn't seen her for years!"

Amelia laughed. "I have not spoken directly to my mother. But I sent a message to my brother who discussed it with my mother. There will be four going – my mother, my brother, you and…a cousin."

"When?" I asked.

"At Egg Moon." Amelia said.

"In less than twelve weeks," Master George said. "Before Amelia leaves."

I sat down. Now that these questions were decided, I realized it truly would happen. Those markings on the map were about to become real places.

"You won't be going by boat; you'll be walking instead, at least most of the way, I gather." Master George looked at Amelia for confirmation.

"It is just as well to walk," Amelia said. "My

mother will be meeting people, helping those with sickness and trading information with others. You may need to take a few trips inland, but you should still reach your new fort before the snow flies."

Master George said, "I'll be giving you a letter of introduction and some other messages for the Factor."

"Does he know I'm coming?"

"Yes. Well, he knows he is getting a valuable apprentice. He knows quite a bit. I did not mention – I will in the next message, of course, but I did not, ah, mention that you are, well, not a boy."

"Oh, that is too bad," Amelia put in. "He would be expecting more if he knew."

"Yes, exactly," Master George said quickly, as he stood up. Then he stopped and looked at Amelia as her words sank in. I could not help laughing at his expression. No longer did his gaze slide past her as if she were a tree or a table. As Amelia readied herself to leave fort life behind, she was also shedding the shabby, quiet shadow she had assumed. She stood tall and straight and spoke clearly and directly to everyone, not just to me and the Home Guard. She made jokes in Master George's presence, even contradicted him, and frequently I saw his eyes stop on her, as if only now had they met.

Amelia and I sat for a few more moments. After a winter of enforced routine, the abruptness with which my life was to change took some adjustment. Amelia was working on an ornate medallion. It was almost complete. The kitchen was very quiet. Siki was visiting the Home Guard, taking some herbals to an elderly man who was in need of a tonic.

I thought about travelling with Amelia's family. I was anxious about meeting her mother. From what I gathered through Master George and Amelia, she was someone quite formidable.

"Not at all," Amelia protested when I mentioned this to her. "She wants us to do our best, at whatever that is. Sometimes it is hard to do as well as she thinks we could. That is all."

"Perhaps, since I am not her daughter, she will not expect so much."

Amelia bent over her work, trying to hide her smile. "My mother expects everyone to do her best, not just her children. So prepare yourself."

She relented when she saw my expression. "You will be fine, Willa. She will not expect you to do more than you can. Do not worry so much!"

"I wish you were coming with us," I said.

Amelia sighed. "I wish so too." She paused and looked carefully at her work. "But I must be sure that Siki is settled. My family will meet me on their return. Then we will celebrate."

GOOSE MOON: APRIL, WHEN THE GREY GEESE APPEAR

As the day I was to leave drew nearer, I began to worry in earnest. I knew York Factory, I knew Master George, I knew the men and my work. Why had I agreed to go into this strange, dreadful wilderness to work somewhere far removed from what little I knew? Why was I leaving the life I had made for myself? How would I manage? How could I make the long journey that gave even Master George nightmares? I began to wonder if it would not be much easier simply to marry him. But when I began to contemplate it, I would hear my mother's voice, lamenting her inability to care for us after her husband's death. I wanted to care for myself, and should not need someone to look after me as if I were a child. In her last days, even with her last breath, she had exhorted me to learn this lesson. Or I would hear Charles say, "You'll follow the footsteps of famous explorers! Perhaps see a buffalo! Or ride in a canoe!" He would not understand my fears. He would want me to go and be proud of it. And I would think of Amelia, who was so strong and brave, and her wistfulness at not being able to come with us. She obviously felt I was lucky to be going. Lucky!

After all, I would console myself, I would be well protected on my trip. Protected from what, I was not entirely sure. Other than Master George's evasive remarks and odd behaviours by some of the men, I was not sure what to expect. My worries ebbed and flowed. Because our travel would be south and west, at least it would be warmer longer, and more things could live and grow.

I was also not happy about leaving Master George before the busy season, but he told me not to worry. Someone would arrive either by ship or from another fort, as planned, to replace me. "Although you were a fine – nay, excellent – apprentice," Master George assured me hastily. "Never one better. Perhaps in a year or two, once you've gotten older, you will change your mind and return here. Or perhaps I will move inland."

The idea struck both of us as preposterous, but neither of us laughed. "I may come back," I said.

I would not be present when the ship arrived from England. Others would carry current messages and supplies to the men at the other forts. Even so, though it was months yet before the supply ship would arrive at Five Fathom Hole, preparing for the arrival of the ship held more excitement and anticipation than any other day I had spent at York Factory. The prospect of new faces, new foods, new goods after a long winter spent without was intensely welcomed. The coming of the ship also signalled the closing of summer. From my brief experience, summer here was all too fleeting and winter all too long. Dread and delight were inextricably bound.

For the ship to come, the ice must go. The two facts were inseparable. It took most of the summer before a ship could sail safely through the waters – and icebergs were still a hazard even so.

The sun, so welcome after a season of darkness, had not yet warmed the air. But animals were awakening and returning to our desolate grounds; we cherished each sign of spring's advance.

We watched carefully, however, for the enormous white sea bears, which usually stayed at sea. Occasionally, though, they would come closer. A man was actually chased into the fort by one. The birds, so many of which had flown away soon after my arrival, had returned. Swans, geese, ducks, gulls, and terns filled the ponds and marshes. The honking and quacking were ceaseless. Even a few small songbirds arrived, and falcons and eagles; welcome sights.

FROG MOON: MAY, WHEN THE FROGS CROAK

It was near the end of May when we heard shouts that the ice was going from the Hayes River. Breakup was usually mid-June, but after my first experience of winter at York Factory I was especially glad it was early this year. Master George and I were checking the inventory in the trading house at the time and Master George, with a grand flourish, said, "Our day of spring has arrived. Enjoy!" We stopped by the Home Guard for Amelia and Siki, and then, picking up others on the way, wandered down to the river to watch the huge blocks of ice crash and grind together as they piled up, one atop the other, until part or the whole would break free, and sail gloriously towards Hudson's Bay. We could hardly hear each other over the noise, but we laughed and yelled and pointed to different ice packs bobbing along.

At one point Amelia turned to me and said, excitement in her eyes, "It is almost time! Soon you will leave!"

Master George beside me overheard, and said, in a flat tone, "Yes, that you will." He turned away.

The ice on the land seemed slower to retreat, but the frozen ridges sometimes melted from below, so that an ice-rimmed cap could act as a greenhouse, warming the surrounding air and protecting the lichen and other small plants from the still bitter winds. When out with Amelia, coming across these little bits of life was a treat, and I would sketch them in my book for later study and comparison with Master George's many books of exploration.

Soon the brown, muted earth blossomed with tiny pink, white, purple, and yellow flowers in marshes and on land. Willows grew short and dense along the water's edge. With spring came the dreadful blood-sucking insects, and columns of black flies tormented us relentlessly. Amelia and I began again to pick and dry leaves and stems and flowers. The season, she said, was so short that much must be done quickly. Some she used for medicines; others she added to meals.

We sometimes walked on humpy brown tussocks, a lumpy, awkward walk, but as Amelia would say, come summer these would be dangerous, water filled, bug-infested waters, and we could not walk that way then. With the spring melt, I had tried on my old boots from England to save my moccasins from the wet, but they pinched my feet unmercifully. The past few months had spoiled me with my new warm, flexible footwear, and I abandoned my boots without regret.

Amelia left the fort frequently now, and I went with her as often as I could. She would point out all manner of life and often death – bodies that had been reduced to gnawed bones and the odd feather. We would see wolves or ravens atop a bony mound, and be reminded that, even in death, came life. Still, after our long winter imprisonment, these remains of life, captured by starvation or cold or preyed upon by others, made us thankful for our own breath. Sometimes we would come upon small animals hiding in the brown grasses. They had awoken, like us, from their long season's sleep. We might see a fox, its fur already beginning to change from its blue-grey winter coat into the grey-brown of summer, or a hare, with its ears so much smaller and shorter than the ones I remembered in England.

The ptarmigans stayed all winter. Somehow they were able to find food during the long black cold. The fluffy feathers covering their legs and feet helped them walk in the snow. Their feathers, like the coats of the fox and the hare, were also changing, from a brilliant white to a speckled brown. Often we would startle a snowy owl intent on catching a mouse or a shrew. We saw families of animals popping up everywhere – squirrels, pikas, marmots, and voles. I marvelled at how little I had seen when I arrived the previous year.

By the end of May, the welcoming sounds of water running and dripping from melting ice and snow were constant. With the ground still frozen, however, there was nowhere for the meltwater to go, and so it puddled on the surface. I began to see the merit in the walkways above the gravelly ground. The men were often out examining the buildings, looking for shifting or flooding ground. Everything needed to be raised off the ground to prevent water damage.

EGG MOON: JUNE, WHEN THE BIRDS SET

With spring and renewed preparations for the coming trading season came also the arrival of many of the Home Guard and Amelia's family. I took heed that Amelia had done her best to ensure my journey would not be a misery nor end in tragedy. From Amelia's reminiscences, I knew that summer was a terribly busy time for her family. They crisscrossed the land providing counsel, critical information, and other assistance to many in need of such. I did not know, therefore, how she was able to arrange for her mother to take me to the new fort, but I could see it was a great comfort to her and to Master George to know Moon was to be my guide. Apprehensive though I still was, I knew if they were reassured, I should be too. For their sakes and my own, I tried hard to seem ready, if not eager, to travel.

Her mother did not come to the fort, but she sent a message that they were nearby. Master George had told me that Moon guided only her own people now, and that I should be grateful and appreciative of this rare opportunity. I could see he thought it reflected well on him that Moon had agreed to take his apprentice after refusing people of importance. However, I also knew very well that Moon had agreed to guide me because her daughter had asked her to, not because of anything George had said.

Amelia and I met Miki Siw at one of the sun-dappled lodges outside the fort walls. The three of us stood while I was reintroduced to him, and then he gave us a formal message from Moon, their mother. "Greetings, Misiwâpos, my daughter. Rather than meet you in haste, I would wait until our gathering in four moons' time. There I will be able to say what is in my heart about your long absence from me. For now, my thoughts are with you and I count the days until you are with us once more."

Amelia did not seem surprised. Instead, equally formally, she said to Miki Siw, "Give my mother my greetings. I too count the days until we are together. My friend who travels with you is ready. She will be no trouble on your trip."

Then she poked Miki Siw in the stomach.

"Don't eat all the food on the way there, you!"

He smiled and said, "Did you make the pemmican? Then I will be sure to have plenty at the end." Then he sobered. "It is hard for Mother to be so close and yet not see you."

Amelia looked downcast. "It is her choice. She still must think I was wrong to come here. Even I think I made a mistake. She has lost all respect for my judgement."

"That is not true!" Miki Siw protested. "You have given us much valuable information. And look at all those people you have helped. They would have suffered much without you. And then there is Kino...." He trailed off.

Amelia looked unconvinced.

"You know how she is," Miki Siw said weakly.

"Has she spoken to you about me? In all the time I have been away?"

Miki Siw hesitated.

"She has not, has she?"

"No. But that does not mean...."

"*Ehe*. It means nothing." Amelia said quietly. "Go with care. And watch over my friend." She turned and smiled at me. "I plan to visit you soon, once you are settled in the new fort."

I cleared my throat and said, after a couple of false starts, "When do we leave?"

"Tomorrow. Before first light," Miki Siw said.

"I will wake you," Amelia said. "Tonight, though, we have your party."

I groaned. "A party? Who will be there?"

"Anybody who can walk or crawl," Amelia teased. "The Home Guard is preparing a feast. I can hardly wait!"

"Perhaps your mother will come to that?"

Amelia looked questioningly at Miki Siw. He shook his head. "She plans to gather a few herbs for the journey."

There was an awkward pause, then Amelia said, too brightly, "George wants to say a few words tonight."

"I hope he finishes before we must leave," Miki Siw joked. "I would like some sleep." We all laughed.

For the party, each dwelling had prepared a different kind of food, and Amelia, Siki, Miki Siw, and I wandered casually from fire to fire. Clouds of mosquitoes and flies hummed vengefully just outside the circle of smoke. Master George, speaking after we had all eaten, kept his speech uncharacteristically short. He hoped, he said, that I would return, but until that time he wished me Godspeed and good health. Everyone applauded and cheered. The fires started to blow and spark as the wind picked up, and I felt a chill. I moved in closer to the flames and caught a glint of metal. Standing just outside the rim of light the fire threw was Dyer, immaculately attired, as usual.

He was smiling, but not at me. His attention was focused intently and entirely on Amelia, who was standing next to me. She did not look his way, but her arm went protectively around Siki, who was laughing and talking to Miki Siw on her left. I did not know why Dyer persisted in his attentions to Amelia, nor why he spoke so kindly to Siki and presented her with trinkets when Amelia was present, yet seemed not to see her when Amelia was absent. Perhaps he took pleasure in raising Amelia's ire, since she ignored and avoided him otherwise. Only lately had she begun to let her contempt for him show, but that, if anything, seemed only to spur him on.

Siki had been working hard, often coming late to our room or sometimes not returning at all. She went all over the fort, often to the Home Guard, it seemed, and would return to us exhausted, her eyes red-rimmed. She stopped asking Amelia for help, saying merely that she had to learn to deal with her work herself. Amelia and I would exchange wondering glances – this bustling, industrious woman was hardly the timorous Siki we had known such a short time ago. But even though Siki now seemed to be firmly in control of her duties, Amelia still seemed troubled. I would see her watching Siki uneasily. But she spoke none of her fears to me.

I had already given Master George some of my sketches of plants and birds I had observed not far from York Factory. He had accepted them graciously but with few words, though he showed me later the leather portfolio he had carefully stowed them in. I noted that he kept it on the shelf with his favourite books, and I was pleased.

I had not known what to offer Amelia. She had given me so much and seemed to need so little in return. Finally, after much thought, I presented her with a drawing of herself, one I had done at a time when she was lost in merry thought, looking westward away from the Bay, recalling her true life. I had worked carefully and long on it afterwards, using plant dyes for colouration. Though small in size, the likeness was quite remarkable; her lovely spirit bright.

"We will see each other too soon for gift-giving

now," Amelia said laughingly, though tears were in her eyes. "And with all the packets George has for you, it is just as well! But…I have one gift for you also, but do not worry – it is light. Light as air. Can you guess? No?" Amelia hugged me and continued, "It is a story, one I have made just for you. And when you are sad and miss your kindred, I hope you will repeat this story to yourself and remember that I am your sister, and that you have family in this land." My friend told me a story about a young woman alone in the world who sailed across an ocean to a special place….

)) ◆ ((

After all the conversations and planning, my actual leave-taking was perfunctory. Amelia, excited for me, was anxious to see us begin our travels. Master George gave me the packet of letters, the map, and other small items. I carried a packsack containing a blanket, my vest, two spare sets of moccasins and leather to mend them, a bundle of pemmican, a knife, an awl, sinew for thread, and other sundries.

Amelia had finished her painstaking work on the medallion: a tiny, breathtaking scene that began at the outer edges and continued, in ever-smaller spirals, telling a story to Amelia's mother. While I did not know the story nor the meaning of the many symbols, the sheer intricacy, the subtle shadings of colour, the invisible, minute stitchings, made me more anxious about its safekeeping than the packet of precious mail Master George had supplied me with.

"I think my quillwork has improved over the years," was all Amelia would say, when I would admire her skill. "I hope my mother thinks so too."

Miki Siw and Master George, who had been closeted together until early in the morning, appeared at the doorway and came towards us.

Amelia hugged me, whispering, "Safe journey."

Master George, after a moment, also hugged me. "Remember what I've told you." I nodded. He had recently warned me about every possible contingency. If I didn't fall off a cliff, drown, starve, get murdered in my sleep by some stranger, or break a limb and be left for dead, who would be more surprised?

"I hope to see you both again…some day," I said.

Within a short time, Miki Siw and I were out of the fort, past the Home Guard, and on our way.

MOON

My first sight of Amelia's mother, Moon, came when she and a boy stepped directly in front of us, seemingly from nowhere. I shrieked and jumped back. Moon graciously ignored my behaviour. She smiled. "Willa. I have heard many good things about you. You are welcome to walk with us." Her English was very slightly accented. Her teeth, like Amelia's, were astonishingly white and even. Amelia had insisted it was due to the small green twigs that she used daily to brush her teeth. Moon's hair was long, black, and plaited. Her clothing was simple leather leggings, a tunic, and knee-high moccasins. The fronts of the moccasins were deep blue and white.

"I am pleased to meet you," I said. "I am honoured you will be taking me to the new fort on the Kisiskachiwun River."

She inclined her head in reply. "My own name is difficult for you to say. So you may call me Moon." She turned slightly to the boy who stood beside her, and I looked at him fully for the first time, and then stepped back in surprise.

"You!" I said.

It was Kino Sesis, Amelia's cousin. He stood with his legs apart and his arms folded. He did not look at me.

"You remember Kino's face, then," Moon said. "We were not sure you would. It is just as well."

Kino said something I couldn't understand.

"We will be practising our English speaking," Moon said. "You may need to remind us if we forget and speak a different language."

I looked at Kino. I knew he could speak English well.

Kino said, "I wouldn't know her. They all look the same to me."

Miki Siw shifted beside me. "He means it as a joke, Willa. We hear that about us."

I smiled and said, "Of course. I understand." I started to take off my pack, saying to Moon, "I have something to give you from Amelia...a gift."

"You may give it to me at one of our stops. We should walk during daylight. But you seem to have a heavy load," Moon observed. "You are unused to walking long, I think. Why don't you let me carry the sack?"

I realized, for the first time, that I was the only one with a big sack. The others carried one small leather bag slung over a shoulder. Kino and Miki Siw each had arrows, and all three carried knives with carved handles and curved bone and copper blades.

"Aren't you carrying any food? Blankets? Won't it be cold at night?"

Kino made a derisive sound. Moon ignored him, saying instead to me, "We are travelling light. We should be able to find what we need along the way. We all have pemmican, of course," she gestured to the leather bag, "because it will save us from having to stop and hunt constantly. We will build a shelter each night."

"I should be able to carry my sack. It's not too heavy."

"As you prefer," Moon said. "It was wise of you to bring such a large pack. I hope to gather some roots along the way, and perhaps I would be able to keep some in there."

"Certainly," I said.

We set off along the Hayes River. Amelia and I had walked that way many times before, and so I knew it would be hard. Because the ground was so soft and wet in places, we sometimes had to detour inland. It wasn't long before my feet and legs were tired and my back ached from carrying the pack. I tried to keep up, and Moon or Miki Siw would often drop back and walk with me, but Kino was soon so far ahead that he was out of sight. Since the land was flat and virtually treeless, I thought this was quite a feat.

Finally, Moon called a halt. I was hot and tired, hungry and thirsty. My feet and leggings were soaked, and the incessant humming of insects was punctuated only by their stings. We stopped near a jumble of rocks on the riverbank. Moon got down on her stomach and cupped her hands to drink. After a moment, I pulled off the packsack and did the same. It was so cold and sweet. When I was done, Moon was watching me. "You stay here, Willa. I will gather something to eat. We rest here for a time."

I limped over to my pack and flopped down. Following Moon's example, I had removed my moccasins and walked barefoot through the bogs and water. My feet were toughened from the spring excursions with Amelia, but I was unused to the rapid pace they set without a break. The air shifted around me, and I watched the butterflies and bees flutter from leaf to blossom. A dark purple, fragrant little flower seemed the favourite. Yellow poppies bent their heads on thin stems, and I saw tiny white blossoms that reminded me of Lily of the Valley from England. After a few moments, I realized I was alone. Had Miki Siw gone with Moon? I had been too tired to notice. I heard a slight sound and turned quickly. It was Kino. He looked furious.

"Get up! It is not time to stop! Where are they?"

I scrambled up and pointed into the bushes. "In there. She – Moon went to get something."

Kino grunted. He moved over to the river and stood watching it.

"How is your arm?" I ventured, after a moment's silence.

"Fine," he said, without turning.

"The men at the fort are still looking for you. After the man died –"

"He died from a sickness, not because of me."

"I know."

Kino gathered some pebbles from the bank and skipped them, one at a time, into the current. They bounced five, even six times, before disappearing under the water. He glanced at me sideways. "It was fitting he died after taking my knife."

"I didn't like him either."

"He said they were going to chop us down, like so many trees." Kino brought his arm down in a harsh movement.

I stared. "Who? You? Your family?"

Kino glared at me. "All of us. All of us who live here."

I looked at the wilderness surrounding us. "But…how could he?"

"He cannot, now."

"But others don't think as he does."

Kino said nothing. I caught a flicker of movement and suddenly Miki Siw was beside me.

"Why are we stopping so soon?" Kino asked him.

"There is a good supply of tufty heather here." Miki Siw squatted down and said to me, "It is a good tinder. Could I take your sack? We could put some in the top to dry as we walk."

I handed him the packsack. "Be back soon," he said over his shoulder.

Kino grumbled and started after him. I was left alone again. The river swished rapidly past, birds twittered in the trees, and the sun was warm. I stretched, feeling sleepy, but I stood reluctantly. Without the packsack on my back, I felt much better. I started after Kino and stopped abruptly. There was no path. No way of telling exactly which way he had gone. In fact, other than the jumble of rocks a foot from me, there was no sign that I could see of where they had gone or even from where we had come. What if they did not return? I could die here. Slowly I made my way over to the rocks and sat down to wait. I no longer had a desire to sleep.

After an interminable time they reappeared. Moon was wearing the sack. "Ready to go?" Moon asked. "I will carry the pack for a short while, *ehe?*"

I nodded, unable to speak.

The beautiful day stretched on mercilessly. I had stopped looking around and instead watched the backs in front of me, then just their feet. Even so, when they stopped I walked into them. It was dusk.

"Here we will stop for the night," Moon announced. Kino and Miki Siw immediately set about gathering deadfall, while Moon worked at building some kind of a shelter. After a moment, I searched also and added wood to the growing pile. Miki Siw disappeared into the woods. Moon handed Kino some small tightly-compacted balls of dried moss for tinder. Kino had a black stone that he used as flint and another kind that he used as steel and soon he had a fire burning cheerfully. Miki Siw came back with a limp bundle that he skinned, chopped, and skewered onto long, thin tree branches stripped of their leaves. My pack was leaning against a shrub, and I hastened over to retrieve the little tin pot Master George had provided me with. By the time I had filled it with water and carried it over to the fire, I saw that Moon had already set a leather bag into the glowing logs at the edge. It was full of water. I hesitated by the fire.

"Oh, you have a pot!" Moon said. She was wrapping roots in leaves and placing them near the leather bag. The wood snapped and crackled. "Could we cook the water parsnips in the pot?" She left the ones that had already begun to steam in their wrappers of leaves and added a few white spheres to my little pot. Then she hung the pot by its handle on a long green branch Miki Siw gave her and propped the pot on two forked sticks stuck in the ground above the fire. She smiled at me. "Would you like tea?"

Tea! I had forgotten to bring tea. "Do you have some?" I asked.

Kino sniffed in an exaggerated fashion and looked around.

"We do," Moon said. "Do you have a cup?"

I did.

She had three flattened little birch cups that were coated in some waterproofing substance, I assumed. She opened them into little cup shapes, and poured tea for the three of them. I handed her my heavy cup. Miki Siw and Kino, meanwhile, had been roasting little bits of meat and handed us each a hot morsel. There was no cutlery or plates, so we ate them directly off the twig. The parsnips were lifted off the fire and we skewered each one with a green twig and ate them. They were sweet and delicious. The tea was a mixture of mint leaves and Labrador tea, Moon told me. I belatedly understood from Kino's hint that the fragrant tea was from the small shrubs with reddish leaves and white flowers that I had noted on our way to this camp spot. The mint was, of course, familiar to me.

It was night. I was exhausted. The fire burned low. I remember Moon showing me the shelter. My blanket was on top of a layer of shrubby boughs and moss. I crawled in, wrapped the blanket around me, and knew no more until dawn.

MOULTING MOON: JULY, WHEN BIRDS MOULT THEIR FEATHERS

The days merged into weeks, spring turned into summer. The nights were no longer so cold. Moon assured me that it would get even warmer as we moved farther south. After having been accustomed to a virtually treeless land, we began to see a gradual change. The trees remained spindly, but were taller and of different kinds. Now we saw trees I was familiar with from home – pine and fir and spruce – and then ones that lose their leaves come autumn – larch, aspen, birch. Moon said that we would soon be in forests so thick that they would block the sun. After the barren Hudson's Bay, this would be something to see.

The ground was no longer so spongy and wet,

although we still had to skirt boggy areas. It meant we could walk farther, if not necessarily longer. I had brought too much for the journey, and the pack was heavy. At various times Miki Siw, Moon, and even Kino carried it, but no one said a word to me about its weight or bother. I still carried Amelia's gift to her mother, still ungiven, inside the pack. Moon was waiting until we reached a certain spot before she would accept it.

I would hear frogs and toads trilling as a signal of water, and then the call of the redwinged blackbirds. While collecting cattail heads to dry out and use for tinder later, we might glimpse a brown shape on a boggy shore – a moose or a bear. Even roses sometimes grew in these wet areas with simple, five-petalled blossoms. The fragrance and the thorns recalled the ones of home.

Things did not always go smoothly, however. One day, while walking at a comfortable pace, my back, legs and feet having adjusted somewhat, Kino brushed past me and went straight up to Moon, who was a bit ahead of me.

"She's eating all the pemmican! There won't be enough to last the rest of the journey. What is the matter with her?"

I stopped walking, aghast. I'd assumed I was carrying my share of the food, and I was constantly hungry and thirsty. Sometimes I felt I could eat forever, and still not be full, and yet I was eating more than I ever had in my life. What was I thinking, though? Obviously they weren't eating nearly as much, and the pemmican was the kind of food that was hard to quit eating, it was so good. I had quickly grown to love its flavour. I had been selfish, though.

I could feel myself flush and I stood downcast, awaiting Moon's admonishments. That she was angry I could tell. She had her left hand on her hip. Amelia had told me that was a signal that she was very angry indeed. I pulled out the leather ball filled with pemmican and offered it to her.

"I – I'm very sorry," I said. "It's so good I guess I've been eating it without really realizing it." She looked at the parcel; there appeared to be a fair bit left, but then I wasn't sure how much longer we'd be travelling. Perhaps there wasn't enough left and they would have to share their portions with me. That would explain why Kino was so upset.

"Put it away, Willa," Moon said gently. Then she turned to address Kino. "Willa is our guest, Kino. She is unused to our way of life, our way of eating. Even if it were all gone, then I would not have been very surprised. But as you can see, she has plenty left for the trip, so you needn't worry." She ever so slightly stressed the word "worry." "Did you know George Talk traded a great deal to make sure there was enough for us all on this trip, not just for Willa? You should thank her for your share of this excellent pemmican."

Kino looked angrily at me, and then back at Moon.

I felt great relief that Moon was not angry with me. I had done nothing terribly wrong. We each had our own food supply.

Then Kino said, respectfully, "Aunt, you are right. Her ways are different from ours. I did not want her to run out of food, but I see Talks Too Much made sure she had plenty, which is lucky for her."

Moon's lips tightened. "George Talk was generous and fair with us all, Kino. We all received the same amount, as you know. Is your supply light? I will be happy to share mine with you."

I held my leather ball out. "You're welcome to some of mine, also."

Kino made a startled gesture. "No, Aunt. You need not. I did not know." He bowed his head to his aunt before striding between us, with one more furious glance thrown my way as he passed.

Moon turned to me and touched my shoulder. "He is young yet. Please forgive his words."

)) ● ((

One night when we stopped early, I pulled out one of the leather-bound journals Master George had given me. I had the map folded carefully inside. I traced the route from the Hayes River to Lake Winnipeg and then on to the Kisiskachiwun River. Since we had moved inland, I wasn't sure where we were in relation to the drawing. Master George had told me that one of Moon's terms had been that she and I would avoid all forts – whether owned by the French or the English. I didn't ask why. Master George, although disappointed, had agreed to this, although it meant I would be taking mail to Edmonton House, the new fort on the Kisiskachiwun River, but not to any others.

"Is that your map?' Kino asked, pausing for a moment in his gathering of deadfall. He squatted beside me. "What is this supposed to be?"

"That's to show the waterfalls at some junction."

Kino snorted. "And this?"

"Those are mountains."

"And here? Is this supposed to show the river through the grasslands? That is not right." He turned and gestured to Miki Siw. "Cousin, come see this."

Miki Siw, who had been preparing my shelter, brushed the bark and twigs from his clothes and walked towards us.

"Here," Kino pointed.

Miki Siw leaned down and looked closely at the spidery marks on the paper. He traced the route from the fort along to where Kino's finger was tapping the map.

"Well, in a year with much rain, then the river does turn there. But then here, this is often flooded, but it shows land. Those are mountains, I think. And it shows some portages. But what is this?"

"I think the mapmaker wasn't sure what was along that part."

Kino laughed. "So what are you supposed to do when you get there? Does everything vanish?"

I smoothed out the paper on my knees. "I didn't think we were going that way. This map only concerns itself with the route to the new fort, Edmonton House."

Moon appeared beside us. She carried a limp goose under her arm. She set it gently beside Miki

Siw and crouched down. "A map? Could I see?"

I moved the map so that she could see it more easily. She brushed at a stain that had obscured a corner of the map.

"Watch out, Aunt," Kino said, "you might tear the map and then we would be lost!" he started to laugh, but quieted when no one paid him any attention.

"I think more than one made that map," Miki Siw said to Moon. "See here, where the river runs...and here...." He pointed out a few areas on the map.

"Yes," Moon mused as she pored over the tracings. Finally she turned to me and said, "Your people rely a great deal on drawing words and pictures on paper. Does no one have a long memory?"

Kino jumped up and began stacking the deadfall. He had large seedpods that he pressed open, and he pulled out the soft white fluff for tinder.

"Some of us do, but maps and books...they record information for others who have not been to a place themselves. It is a way to record events."

"We know what they're for," Kino said, as he arranged twigs and bark in a conical shape.

"We draw some ourselves, if we need to help someone," Miki Siw explained.

"We just don't carry them commonly," Moon said. "This map, for instance. As Miki Siw says, it is not right in places. And even if it were right one year, it would not necessarily be right the next. And here it is not right at all, because if the river were that high, then the land here would be covered. And this part here cannot be walked. It is so wet that you would sink up to your neck if you tried to walk it, yet it is too solid to float a canoe on."

"Well, there was a more detailed one, but I didn't have time to trace it. But even so," I said, folding up the map carefully, "we are not following the marked route anyway."

"No. A piece of paper cannot decide things for you. You must look, think, and then decide." Moon gestured to the journal I had on my knees. "That book you have there, where you are drawing pictures of plants." I nodded. I had been making notes on plants that Amelia and her mother collected. Moon took the journal from my knees and opened it to a page seemingly at random.

"This is a very good picture of bear berry. These marks here might say something about it being good for tea, or to smoke or to help with stomach problems. *Ehe?*"

"*Ehe* – yes," I said, nodding again.

"And you could draw another picture of it with its white and pink flowers, and another when it is dried, and another showing a similar plant but not quite the same. And this would help others who had not seen it know what it looked like. Yes?"

"Yes."

"But would it not be better to be able to see the living plant, to learn where it grows, and to have someone show you how to use it, how to prepare it, and when it should be used?"

"Certainly," I said.

Moon handed me my journal and leaned back, wrapping her hands around her knees. "My son has told me of the room George Talk has. Full of these big books. Stacked up above his head." Moon shook her head. "Our people teach others these things. We do not use books. Books and maps are so important to your people, but they still do not keep you from getting lost or help you find food or live on this earth."

"What do you do?" I asked.

"We listen to our people. We learn. We teach others how to think. Not *what* to think but *how* to think. The young learn from the older and wiser. They also learn things you might write in a book – when to pick the plants for healing, when to travel, what animals are good to eat, what ceremonies to hold. Our world changes. We must always learn. If we do not learn and use properly what we know, then we may die. But the old can also learn from the younger. My daughter is at that place not only to learn, but also to teach. She uses what she learns, and she thinks of new ways of doing things."

"We have that too. Sort of." Of course, as a girl I had not been apprenticed to anyone. Until coming here, that is. And the purpose of apprenticing is to pass on information, albeit as a very thin thread of life.

"You travel light," I said. "You couldn't carry heavy books anyway."

"That is right," Moon said approvingly. "And even if we wanted to –"

"Which we don't –" Kino put in.

"Then what would happen if they got wet? Or stained? Or lost? Then what would we have to rely on? If you begin to think knowledge is only outside you and you do not look and think and learn for yourself, then you will forget what you know. You will not look around you at what is; you will look at what someone else has said should be. Do you understand?"

Kino hopped up and began to stagger around,

a vacant look on his face. "Where am I?" he said, "I thought I was here on the map, but it just doesn't look like that mark!"

I laughed in spite of myself.

"It is inside here," Moon said, tapping her head. "You must learn to carry what you must know inside. There it will not get wet or lost. It will be with you at all times and it will be easy to carry."

"And the knowledge is passed on to someone else?"

For the first time since we had met, Moon looked old and tired. "That is how it used to be. Not so long ago." She paused, rubbing arcs in the dirt with her moccasin. "Now the pattern is changing." She looked down and saw the dead goose sitting there. Slowly she rose and took it near some bushes where she started plucking it, setting some of the longer feathers into a separate pile.

Kino went back to tend the fire.

"What does she mean?" I asked Miki Siw, who remained.

"Sickness. *Omikewin* – the pox. New diseases. So many of our old ones have died. Then their trained ones have died. It is happening so fast and so often that there is not time to pass on all the wisdom of the elders. We try to save as much as we can, but…." He waved a hand at my journal. "It would be as if your books had only one or two pages remaining, and the rest all torn out. As if you knew only the beginning and the ending, nothing in the middle."

"Then you do need books. You need someone to write all this down before it is too late."

"You have all the words of wisdom from the beginning of your time? Everything is written down?"

I shook my head. "Much has been lost, or burned, or damaged in some other way."

"No. Even if it were possible, which it is not, that is not the answer for us. No."

"I know the answer." Kino rose from his place at the fire, and this time he was not smiling. "Get back in your big ships and sail off. And stay away!"

Miki Siw ducked his head. "We know you are not going to do that," he said. "But many of our people are now staying far from your people. Bad things seem to follow when we meet with you."

"But what about the goods we have given you? The pots? The blankets? The guns?"

Kino looked around us in an exaggerated fashion. "Well, what would we do without all that?

How did we manage all those seasons without you?"

"We like to travel light," Miki Siw reminded me.

I realized then that they had nothing, nothing at all, that came from York Factory. I was the only one who carried any goods from England.

KISKINO HUMAKEWISKWEW – TEACHER

After this conversation, Moon began to ask me, when I would look at a plant she had gathered, what I could tell her about it. At first I was at a loss for words. What could I say about a plant I had never seen before? The first time this happened, Kino appeared from somewhere and said slyly, "Look in your book. Oh, it's not there? Too bad. Now what will you do?" and then he went off.

Moon then asked me to describe it as a way to tell her something. "Does it look like another plant you have seen? Think."

It did, and I told her that.

"And do you know where that plant grows?

Not exactly where, just what kind of place might you find it? And what do you know about that plant?"

In this way I was able to gain knowledge of a great number of plants as we went along, both useful to us and yet interesting in their own right. A time came when I could reel off names and attributes of a great number of plants. I had pages in my journal describing them. But as Moon would constantly remind me, "Knowing the names means nothing. You could call it any name. Applying what you know is more important."

She also warned me about assuming that if a plant had two or more attributes similar to another, it would have other properties in common. As we went along she would show me almost identical plants, like hemlock and deer parsnip, yet one would be poisonous while another would be a useful medicinal herb. One carelessly picked and dried plant could cause serious harm.

As time passed the trees and shrubs and plants began to sort themselves into recognizable groups. While I had no real idea where I was, or what would await me at the end of my trip, or even whether I would make it there alive, I felt cheerful upon waking, and looked forward to the day's events.

MÂKWA – LOON

One night we made our camp alongside a large lake. As we finished our preparations for the night and took our places beside the fire, we heard haunting cries coming from the lake. "What animal is that?" I asked Moon.

"Did you not see *mâkwa* at the fort?" Moon asked, surprised.

I shook my head.

"I'll show you," Miki Siw said, and he and I went down to the lake's edge. There, swimming gracefully by twos, were elegant black and white birds. A mist hung near the trees on the far shore and the water, a clear, cold blackness, was calm.

"Look closely," Miki Siw whispered and, waving his arm slowly over the water's edge, he scattered some pebbles into the water. We watched as one bird swam closer. The others almost imperceptibly changed course away from us.

"See the white necklace," Miki Siw pointed out, "and the eye?" The bird, large, graceful, and cautious, regarded us through its red jewelled eye. It came quite near. Then its mate called from across the lake, and this one responded in kind before gliding back to her.

For some reason, their mournful cries recalled my family. After our silent return to the fire, I sat brooding on the unhappy events of my past. I pulled the locket out from around my neck and regarded my mother's and brother's likenesses until darkness fell. My bleak thoughts were interrupted by Moon's quiet voice. She told us a story, a story of the Loon's Necklace, for that was the name of the birds we had seen. It took me away from my melancholy remembrances, and I was able to set aside my cares for another time.

When Moon was finished her tale, I gave her my thanks. "I have missed hearing stories."

"Does no one tell them where you come from?" Moon asked.

"Oh, long ago, my family did. But then our lives grew too hard for stories."

"Too hard? That is a good time for them," Moon said. "To remind us of better times, different times."

I smiled. "Amelia told me many good stories. We laughed so much. She said she had heard many from you."

For a moment Moon's usually serene expression changed. "Mine? My stories are not very funny. The younger ones seem to like those ones."

Miki Siw spoke up. "My mother knows many important stories. About our people, about our lives long ago, about things to come."

"Yes, Amelia told me stories about those things. About how the earth was made, about the Great Spirit. She told me some about Trickster...."

"And Hare? And Buffalo?"

"Yes, those, but the ones I liked best were about the sun dogs and the north lights."

"Have you heard the one about the Trickster in the mountain pass?"

I shook my head. And from that night forth, before retiring for the night, one of us would tell a story. Kino loved to tell jokes. Miki Siw's tales were often solemn, even sad, while Moon's stories were rich in detail, vivid and textured. They were interested in hearing about London too and about religion, although it was difficult to explain certain things and they often laughed at the serious parts and were pensive at funny things. Still, I think we all hoped it would be Moon who would take a turn once night fell and we were sitting at the fire. As darkness closed in, her soft voice could conjure up the most fabulous visions. It helped me forget for awhile the fact that I was in a wilderness where mistakes could lead to the death of me or others by many different means. I could forget that, but for them, I would be surrounded by wilderness and without the ability to find my way back to civilization.

ÔSIH – CANOE

The rivers we saw, since they all flowed to the Hudson's Bay, often had people in canoes floating silently and swiftly in that direction, although at this time of year their destination would be somewhere other than the Bay. We even saw a couple of York boats containing furs and men, but no one wished to speak with them.

"We would help if needed. But they are doing fine," Moon would explain, as we watched the boats pass us by, seemingly unaware of our presence.

Moon was highly sought after by her own people and other tribes almost from the time we left York Factory. They would ask Moon and Miki Siw for news and other information. If required,

Moon would also give out herbs with instructions for use. Some were for illness, others were for wounds. Sometimes there would be ceremonies and speeches before Moon would learn what they wanted. They would give us food or other useful knowledge in return. Moon and Miki Siw would then pass on messages to other groups we would meet along the way.

After seeing the Home Guard and Amelia's manner of dress, I had assumed all in this land would wear similar attire and hold similar beliefs. Knowing how different people were in different parts of England, I became ashamed at having thought all would be like here. On our travels we occasionally met some whose rituals and beliefs were very foreign to me. Moon would direct Kino Sesis and me to restrict our movements and stay together when we approached these strangers. I saw many unusual things. But when I became too afraid and thought I might panic, I would think of Charles and his inexhaustible curiosity. I would think of Moon's teachings. "Learn," I would say to myself. I watched closely when Moon and Miki Siw spoke with these people. I thought of how I would paint them, and I studied their faces and attire and belongings. By concentrating on finding things out, I found I could contain my fear and not run away.

Sometimes we came upon tragic situations. The Small Pox had raged and killed many here ten years previously. The disease still killed now, of course, but in smaller numbers than before. Twice we came upon young children who had been spared the Pox but were the only ones left of their band. We would find them living a sadly reduced existence, with no one to teach or care for them. They were fearful of us and had hidden themselves, yet Moon or Miki Siw would see them and coax them out. Moon would share food with them, and wait until they were ready to share their stories. On both occasions these children travelled with us until Moon found suitable families, ones who greeted our travellers joyfully and adopted them as their own sons and daughters.

We had a more varied diet on that journey than we ever had had at the fort, perhaps because we were so few and the specialties would go farther, or possibly because there was so much more game and crops to choose from and trade for. We were given corn and hazel nuts and even plums. Miki Siw told me they had been traded with a tribe who lived near mountains in the south. Moon was known to all, and was treated with great respect. Her words were heard with solemnity, although she spoke simply and without fanfare.

When I asked Moon about their questions, she would say only that she and Miki Siw travelled constantly, and therefore spoke with many different peoples and heard many useful things. That was why they knew so many of the different customs and interests of different groups, including those of us from across the ocean. "It is hard to remain the same when we meet with so many others," Moon said. "When things are done a different way, you begin to question your own customs. You compare; you must think on which is best. Over seasons, it changes you and your ways. When you return to your own people, you see things differently, and perhaps do things differently, and others see you have altered. But living is change. All things must change, even the stones at our feet."

"Your people must become more like us if you are to live," Kino announced, appearing beside me. "All our people know that."

"To live here they must change," Moon amended. "To live in their own place they may not need to."

"Too bad you did not understand the funny stories about your people," Kino said.

"Like what?"

"Oh, about finding you so sick and weak and

out of food that you cannot walk anymore, or getting lost and stepping in your own footprints." Kino mocked stumbling around in a tight circle. Miki Siw had dropped back to hear, and he laughed.

Kino continued, "Always begging for aid, sitting helpless like babies on the shore when your craft has broken." He rolled his eyes. "Do you remember that time, when we saw those three –" he and Miki Siw paced ahead. Their stride was so long that I had a hard time keeping up and their voices faded away from me.

I glanced at Moon. She seemed to be paying no attention to their jokes. Her eyes were constantly darting around, looking into the woods, ahead of us, beside us. Her stride was also long, but she made an effort not to get too far ahead of me. We had a regular pattern. We were up before dawn, we ate, then we walked.

We were into our journey by about sixty days. It came to pass that, no matter how exhausted I was when I fell into the shelter that each night Miki Siw or Moon prepared for me, I would wake in the pitch dark, unable to see my own hand in front of my face. I had tinder, precious tinder, but lighting it served no useful purpose other than to make the darkness more palpable.

Each night I awoke and lay unable to move, listening to the noises of the night. Stories Master George had told me, about bears demolishing shelters with one swipe of their paws and savaging the victims within, came to me again. I remembered the sea bears Amelia and I had seen when we went out fishing through the ice. Amelia had whispered to me to merely walk onwards, as if we did not see them, neither faster nor slower than before. They may have watched us, but did not attack. We sometimes saw three lying down with their heads close together and their bodies extended to form a three-pointed star. One had followed us for a few moments then left off, to my great relief. Only days later, however, we heard that a man had been attacked and eaten by a sea bear not far from where we had been.

These thoughts came to mind at night as I lay awake. During one of these nearly sleepless times, I could see the moon that had risen while I slept earlier. I watched as a shadow crossed in front of it. It seemed to be moving my way. I sat up and carefully pushed my blanket aside. I grabbed a branch as thick as my wrist, which I had been using as a walking stick, and readied myself in case I was attacked. The shadow grew smaller, then the moon shone clearly once more. Puzzled,

I leaned cautiously out of my shelter. The fire was still burning, not vigorously but steadily. Humanlike silhouettes crouched around it. One was prodding the fire. I gripped my stick a little tighter. One turned, and I recognized Kino.

"Why are you awake?" I called out, astonished.

"Why are you always sleeping?" Kino retorted. "Don't you get tired of lying there all night long?"

I crawled out of the shelter and walked over to where the three of them sat. They always slept in the open near the fire. I, however, was glad Master George had insisted they build me a shelter each night.

"Do you mean you wake up and sit here each night? What for?"

"In colder weather one must sleep light in order to stoke the fire. Or to watch over others. Sometimes after a short sleep one may no longer be tired, and may choose to stay awake for a time," Moon said mildly. She had a roll of leather and was stitching a new sole onto a moccasin in the silvery light. Kino and Miki Siw both had their bows out and seemed to be making new arrows. A small heap of feathers lay between them. I recognized them from the goose Moon had plucked before.

I sat down beside her. "I have been lying awake

in there each night listening to all the sounds, and I never thought it was you three."

"Us? Making noise?" Kino feigned outrage. "You must have heard something else. Like that moose over there." He pointed into the blackness of the trees. I saw nothing. "Or maybe that wolverine." He gnashed his teeth.

Then we all heard a splash.

"Beaver," Miki Siw commented, picking up an arrow and disappearing into the trees.

I shook my head. "Are you truly not tired after walking all day?"

"Tired, yes. So we sleep. But if we wake in the night, sometimes we do not sleep again right away."

"You do go back to sleep then before morning."

"Yes. Did my daughter not awake in the night?"

I thought about it. Amelia was always coming and going. She never seemed to sleep much at any time and then only very lightly. The slightest noise would awaken her. I had assumed that if she'd had a choice she would have stayed in bed. Perhaps not.

In a few minutes Miki Siw was back. "Beaver tail for breakfast!" he announced, holding up the large furry animal. Following Moon's instructions, I skinned the tail while Miki Siw went back to get water to soak it in until morning. Then Moon helped me cut the leather for new soles for my own moccasins. It was quiet, peaceful work. No one said much more. Then, feeling tired and relaxed, I crawled back into my shelter and slept a dreamless sleep.

I awoke to the sun shining through the boughs of my shelter. A cacophony of birds cawed and warbled inches from my ears. I lay back in my blanket, and felt the calm of the morning seep through me. I did not feel the need to rise immediately or to pull the blanket over my head in a desperate attempt to create the illusion of four strong walls surrounding me. I realised, to my surprise, how terrified I had been, and for so long that it had become part of me. It was gone; was it merely because of warm sun shining on my face? No. We had been living out of doors for weeks now, with no wild animal tearing us apart, no crazy men murdering us in our sleep. We had lived and eaten in peace, moving with all the other living creatures in a kind of harmonious life's walk. It was a curious but a very strengthening feeling. I knew no more than on the previous day, and nothing had changed outside myself, yet everything had changed.

FLYING MOON: AUGUST, WHEN THE YOUNG BIRDS FLY

We walked a very long way that day. Moon wanted to reach a certain place by nightfall, and it became a great effort to keep one foot moving in front of the other. We had been going steadily uphill, which seemed to make our movements more difficult. I hadn't seen a place to spend the night along the way, but then each night when Moon would stop she would show me that there was water near, a shelter could be built quite easily, and there was deadfall. Often Miki Siw or Kino would fish. Moon would have gathered herbs and leaves with which to wrap them, and they would be gently steamed or roasted on the fire. They told me some of the bands farther along hated fish and never ate it. Perhaps if they had tried the fish we were eating, then they would have changed their minds.

We feasted also on berries later in the summer – black, blue, red, tart and sweet, big and small. Amelia and I had spent the previous summer gathering and drying berries for the pemmican, and so some were familiar to me. There were gooseberries, raspberries, strawberries, currants, juniper berries, and cranberries as well as other kinds that I hadn't ever seen in England. Here, however, there was a veritable profusion. Animals and insects too were attracted to the fruit. Amelia was daily on my mind. I missed her quick wit and bright laughter, her kindness and warmth. I felt close to Moon and Miki Siw also. They were, like me, more of a solemn temperament. Amelia seemed more like my brother, cheerful and quick-willed. I wondered what her father was like.

The sun was just setting when we finally stopped that night. Moon reached the top of a rise and halted. She looked back at Miki Siw and me; Kino had disappeared as usual. "We are here," she said. I slowly made my way up to her, but I forgot my exhaustion when I looked down the hill. Below us was a grassy plateau encircled by trees. Amongst the grasses, as far as I could see, was a profusion of flowers. Lilies petalled orange, white, and yellow, purple daisies and bee balm and asters, yellow sunflowers with black or brown centres, glorious pink roses. In the centre I could see, like an unblinking eye, a small green pond.

"The flowers are closing now," Moon said, surveying the blooms and breathing deeply. "In the morning, when the sun rises above the trees, you will hardly believe all the colours and smells."

Kino came up behind us, a string of fish slung over his shoulder. "Compare this to your idea of heaven," he said to me. He passed us and set off down the incline.

Moon touched my shoulder. "Tomorrow, you may show me my daughter's gift. This is her special place. I wanted to wait until we reached it to accept her gift."

The next morning I awoke to a new world. Fragrances competed one with another to be foremost in the air; ladybirds and dragonflies vied to catch the most succulent insect. Bees, glittering with colour and heavy from their labours, roved from blossom to blossom.

After our morning meal, Moon listened intently to the words I had memorized for Amelia. She took the medallion from my hands very carefully, as if it were made of china. She studied the minute pictures, following each symbol with the tip of a finger. We all sat silent, watching her. The time stretched on. I leaned back in the grassy meadow to watch tiny jewelled hummingbirds in their magical flight.

Miki Siw finally said, tentatively, "Is she going to come back to our home?"

Moon smiled, her eyes bright in the sun. "She is."

Miki Siw stood and walked over to Moon, then squatted to look at the medallion. After a moment, Kino joined him.

Moon looked at me. "So many of our people are…changed when they have spent a long time with your people. Change is part of life, I know that. But we have lost so many. My daughter carries our old ones' hopes. If even she, who is so strong, wanted to forget our ways…." Moon's gaze fell on the medallion once more. "But she does not."

Kino spoke up. "When we take furs to the fort, that is one thing. We see your people for a few days or sometimes weeks. Then we are back to our own world. With others, working day by day, it is harder."

"My father," Miki Siw said, "he sees bad things. Animals gone. No trees. Thick smoke. He sees our people sick and dead in great numbers, while your people grow and grow."

"That is how it is now," Kino muttered.

"No," Miki Siw said. "It will get worse."

"But my daughter. She will soon be safe with us." Moon put the medallion over her head, slipping it inside her tunic. Then we gathered up our few belongings and started off.

)) ◗●◖ ((

As I walked, almost without plan or thought, merely plodding as a horse or an ox does before the plough, I wondered at the strange turn my life had taken. Here I was in a new land, far from home, my family gone. Could they see me, were they watching over me and happy, or were they shaking their heads at my new life? I thought of Charles in my place. I imagined reading letters sent from him once each year on the supply ship and I knew I would have been happy for him. An adventurous life, which he had always sought...here I experienced some of the very things he had dreamed of. Whenever I was tired or sad and finding my life hard, I would think of him in my place, and it would make it easier to go on.

I would look down at my clothing of furs and leather and remember my mother's excitement when fabric came to be printed in many different designs and the thin, soft material stitched into the latest fashion. I recalled the time it took dressing our hair before we allowed ourselves to be seen in public, the cloth rags we wore to curl it at night. Here I wore my hair as Amelia did, pulled back simply in a plait or pony tail. The strict etiquette and custom-bound perceptions meant nothing here, and the mannered courtesies that had seemed so natural there seemed strained and artificial here, and they fell from me like rain. I did not know their preferred ways, however, and while Moon and Miki Siw accepted without judgement all that I did and said, Kino often seemed to find my behaviour wanting.

As so often happened, what I might ask or say would provoke him. Assuming animals and even plants had been put on earth merely to serve us was one attitude he found particularly aggravating. Moon and Miki Siw would patiently try to explain their way of seeing things, but Kino was more blunt. "Your people can't walk anywhere without our help. You don't know how to live without us. But all other living things on this land live without need of us. What truth can you give that shows you are smarter and more worthy of life than any other living thing?"

Kino was angry when he disagreed with me. Miki Siw and Moon were far more diplomatic, and they expressed their interest in trying to understand me and "our ways." Still, their questions, when stripped of their niceties, amounted to the same criticism as Kino's – why did I believe something or how had I come to any particular conclusion? This questioning served remarkably well at pointing out inconsistencies in thought and action. While I reminded them that I was not a representative of my countrymen and could not explain as well as others could, they persisted in comparing the way they viewed the world with the way I did, and my view, to their minds and increasingly to my own, came up short.

Even so, I began, in what seemed a paradoxical fashion, to feel happier, more sure of myself. Whether they agreed with me or usually did not, they did listen. They did not ask for my brother or my father to speak for me. Because they listened closely, I in turn thought carefully before I spoke. We talked little while walking, of course, and only at night for a time, but during the days of walking I thought a great deal in a way I had not done before.

I had not been my own person in England. Here I was becoming one. I no longer expected, nor wanted, someone to think for me. And the more I thought and made decisions and sometimes fended for myself, the more capable I felt. Of course, I knew I survived here only because of Moon, Miki Siw, and Kino. But they were teaching me well, a bit at a time, and I was learning how to survive. My eyes were opening.

I caught up to Moon one morning. She was carrying my sack again, supposedly to fill it with fresh herbs that, once dried, would be crumbled into a powder and stored in a fine small leather bag. I knew, however, that she was simply being kind.

"Moon," I said, "is this how you always live? Counting on there always being food to pick along the way, and water and shelter?"

Moon continued at the same steady pace. "I don't count on there being food. I have often had to do without. But I plan ahead. I remember from the past."

"But what if you go somewhere you haven't been before? Then what?"

"Then I look around me. I know where certain plants good to eat might grow. I know where water should be. I look at the hills and valleys around me for shelter. I think."

"Still, what if it's been a bad year for plants? What if it snows early, or all the berries are eaten, the animals are gone? People must run into problems."

"We try not to run, but sometimes the young, trying to prove themselves, or the old or the tired, might walk into them."

"So your people make mistakes too."

Moon plucked a long vine and draped it over her shoulder. It was sweet-smelling. "Of course we do. Did you think we did not?"

"Well, no one seems to go anywhere without your people along."

"That is true. But it is a very careful dance to live well in all seasons. Having lived and travelled across this land, we know and can plan more surely than others who have been here such a short time."

We walked in silence for a time. The day was bright and hot. The nights were still warm as August neared its end, and also of a longer duration than at York Factory. The mosquitoes and black flies and tiny, almost invisible insects seemed the same, however, and they encircled me in clouds, day and night. The sun had roughened my skin and browned my arms, but that did not deter them. Whenever we stopped, I would smooth on a poultice Moon made for me.

I was disconcerted at how often George came to mind and, as well, his offer to marry me. I found to my surprise that I missed him and his conversations. George, I thought, was probably missing me as well. So many days he had come looking for me, not because he had a chore for me to do, but merely as an excuse to talk or to have my company while we worked. When I had time away from my work, I sought out Amelia. When George had time from his work, he sought out me. Why hadn't I seen that? Perhaps I just wasn't ready to see it then. I was getting older, I realized, and was learning more about the world and about myself.

I thought about my family many times. Even the treatment of me by my great-uncle, though glad he had seemed to be rid of me, no longer made me sad. I was living a life that would have been impossible for me to lead in London, nor had I even dreamed of wanting this for myself then. Now I saw the door of my small world opening – and I was walking farther away from it each day as I grew stronger and more able to depend upon myself. Where would I be in a year? Who would I be? While thoughts of my brother frequently gave me courage to go on, now I was almost happy to be where I was and to do what I was doing. I began to understand why, if my brother Charles had been the one left alive and sent to Hudson's Bay, that he would think our great-uncle a godsend.

SHEDDING MOON: SEPTEMBER, WHEN THE DEER SHED THEIR HORNS

We had been travelling on foot for many weeks. The land around us had changed again. Here, as we worked our way south and west, the days were long and often hot, even after dark. The trees were no longer short and scrubby. Instead of willows and short spindly spruce, there were tall, sturdy pines and birch. At York Factory the vegetation had turned early to grey and brown.

At Hudson's Bay, there was no time for ornate, luxurious blooms or leaf shapes. The willow's short, narrow leaves, the clinging lichen and moss, the needle-sharp pines – their tenacious but minuscule growth reflected the brevity of the growing season. The animals, of course, matched their home. Even the birds were frequently white, grey, or brown to mirror the season. The snow geese, rock ptarmigan, swans – all were white. They were either silent, or had a short, utilitarian honk. Because of the frequently overcast sky, humid air, and small colour ranges, I had become accustomed to seeing bright oranges, reds, blues, and purples only in the dyes that Amelia made from the roots and stems of different plants or in the strings of beads in the trading house. Here, though, was a riot of colours. Huge leaves of red, orange, and gold loomed above us and on the earth beneath our feet. Tall and short grasses of blue and green and grey rippled like water in the breeze, and blossoms wavered in clumps of colour throughout. During the day, birdsong filled the air and yellow, blue, and red songbirds coloured the skies – skies so bright and blue that I often had to shield my eyes during part of the day. It was a cornucopia for the senses.

As I walked and reflected on my life in London, I recalled how the smoke from the coal-heated homes had obscured the sky from view, and filled the nose with the smell of soot and smoke. When we had had to move from our family home, we went to live in the centre of the city.

There were no trees there or bushes or flowers, only walkways, buildings, and sewage ditches. I had not noticed the smells or the lack of colours then, I had had too many other concerns, but they came back to me now. Here a new sight or sound or fragrance mingled with each step we took. It seemed all jumbled together and I spent much time asking Moon or Miki Siw about what each was.

TIPISKÂW – NIGHT

We were washing in a river one evening. There was no moon and the only remaining light would soon be the fire. As I followed Moon up the bank to our site, she stopped suddenly and turned back. Following her gaze, I saw a canoe silently gliding towards us. In it sat a lone woman. I could see that her face, as she drew up to us, was tattooed in blue, and she wore a woven cap and blanket over her head and shoulders. She spoke inquiringly to Moon. Moon replied, and said to me, "She is looking for me."

She beckoned to the woman to leave her craft and follow us to our site. The woman hesitated, looking at a bundle in the bottom of the boat.

Then she carefully gathered it up and followed us.

Moon led her to the fire and gave her food and drink. Miki Siw and Kino greeted her and made room for them on one side of the fire. I sat beside Miki Siw and watched the two women converse. After some time, the woman brought forth her bundles. The outside coverings were dyed leather. I could not make out the colours from where I sat. As she unwrapped the first bundle, the woman keened softly under her breath. Inside the bundle were long, yellowed, polished bones. The woman stared sadly at them where they lay, neatly aligned in rows. I looked at Miki Siw and Kino. They were watching the woman, but Miki Siw leaned slightly towards me and said quietly, "Her mother."

The bones were carefully rewrapped, and the second, smaller bundle was opened. The bones here were much smaller, obviously from an infant or young child. The woman slowly drew out one white bone and brought it to her cheek before laying it gently back with the rest. The two women spoke together. I saw the shadows cast by the fire on the curve of their skulls. The fire burned low.

After a long while, Moon went to her herbs

and withdrew a large brown nut. She carried it back to the fire. When she opened it carefully, I saw that the inside was filled with a powder. Though the woman held out her hand, Moon did not give her the nut immediately. She replaced the top and they sat, heads bent, over the bones. Moon's voice, and then the woman's, went on and on. My eyes drooped; I stretched out by the fire and fell asleep.

I awoke to the sounds of the fire blazing up. Kino was adding wood. In the west the sky was still dark, but in the east it was turning pink. I looked for Moon and saw she still sat with the stranger, who had bundled up the bones and was staring at the nut she now held. Then slowly the woman shook her head. She handed it back to Moon. Moon smiled, embraced her, and helped the woman to her feet. Miki Siw reverently picked up the bundles and handed them to her. Then the three went through the trees.

Kino spoke to me. "She carries her dead. It is time to leave them at a sacred place, but she cannot bring herself to let them go. But the weight of them is heavy. She wanted my Aunt to help her."

Moon and Miki Siw returned from the river.

"All her family has died," Moon said. "She

thought of joining them once she took the bone people to rest with the others. She is weighed down by them."

The thought of carrying bones around seemed gruesome to me. "Then why does she carry them with her? She must remember without them."

Moon knelt beside me. She touched my neck where the silver locket lay. "It is not the bones themselves that are heavy. Like this necklace, the bones are light. But you carry a heavy burden, even so."

I pulled the locket out. A burden? I regarded my family inside.

Moon leaned closer to study the tiny pictures, the flat colours. "There is a world in there to carry," she said, closing the locket carefully and tucking it back in my tunic. I fingered the chain around my neck. I thought I understood then. My joy, my sorrow, my life was locked up inside something smaller than my thumb. Of course, it wasn't really inside the locket but inside me. But would I want to give up my pictures, even so?

But the bones. That woman had carried bones of her dead. Bones that had carried bodies, people who had breathed and lived through days and nights and seasons. To her those bones once spoke and lived. They really had lived. While I carried only bits of coloured paper. Perhaps it was not so gruesomc.

Moon turned to Miki Siw and Kino. "As we spoke of her mother and her son, they lived for her again. They told her to live. She did not take the powder."

AMELIA

One late afternoon, Miki Siw and Kino were off somewhere and Moon and I were gathering wood. I saw a patch of grass and a heap of twigs under one tree, and when I went over to add them to the growing woodpile, I startled a hare. It leaped out, touched the ground once, and bounded around me, disappearing into the brush on the other side. Seeing the hare reminded me of Amelia, and I said to Moon, "I wonder how Amelia is. She is very worried about Siki."

Moon shook her head. "I was away when the people agreed to send Siki in my daughter's place. I fear for that child. But then, I feared for my daughter and she has done well."

"Amelia said that she was told Siki was the best choice."

"She was the only choice." Moon sighed. "But still she should not have gone. She is not strong. I have bad dreams about her."

"Did you have to send anyone? If there was no one suitable to take her place...."

"My daughter has done such fine work. We have come to rely on her. Some wanted her to stay on, but others said she has completed her time and should be set free again. I was so happy to agree with that."

I threw the load of deadfall in a heap and followed Moon to the river's edge to look for driftwood. "Amelia said you weren't happy with her decision to go."

"I was not!" Moon said fiercely. "My daughter – agreeing to go to that place!" She looked at me apologetically. "I know you don't understand. After all, you went to that place, and here you are going to another. You don't seem to mind. But it seemed to me that my daughter was agreeing to live in a rattlesnake pit. She has so many gifts. I could not bear to lose her."

"But you let her go."

"She said she wanted to go. She thinks well and makes her own plans. My own fear is no good reason to ask her not to go. But it has been hard."

"Well, she knows you think it was a bad idea."

"Not a bad idea. The idea is good. My daughter is very brave. I could not do that, even at my age. But a few seasons ago there were many who wanted to be chosen. My daughter has many abilities that others do not. So why must she be the one to go?"

We walked back up the bank and dumped the wood on the pile. Moon picked up a little birchbark bag she had made along the way and a stout digging stick and handed another to me. We went looking for roots or berries for our meal.

Moon continued, "These past seasons my food has been without taste, my days without colour, my sleep without joy. My husband, my son – it is the same for them. We have had little laughter. But time passes. We wait. Soon my daughter will be with us again."

I stopped, puzzled. "But you could have seen her…even two months past. And Miki Siw was up every year to see her…."

"I could not."

"Why not?"

Moon shook her head. "I could not. I did not want to shame her."

I was incredulous. "Shame her? How? Amelia is very proud of you."

Moon said nothing for a moment and when I looked at her I could see she was struggling to remain calm. When she spoke, however, her voice was as serene and quiet as ever. "I cannot go near that fort. I cannot make my legs walk there. I thought I might meet her where the rivers join, but I was afraid."

Moon picked up her full container, pausing to put a few more roots in my bag. She looked at me and repeated, "I was afraid – afraid I would weep, beg her to come home, tell her how much we need her. I would not want my daughter to feel shame for her weak mother. Therefore, I did not see her."

Miki Siw was at the camp setting up the wood for the fire.

"Amelia would be astonished to hear you," I commented.

"Why?" Moon said.

"She thought that you felt her judgement was poor. That you would not see her because you were ashamed of her."

Moon stood still. "Poor judgement? My daughter? She has always been smarter and stronger than I. The work she has done in her short life...."

Moon appealed to Miki Siw. "How could she think that, my son? Did you not tell her how we missed her presence? How dark our lives are?"

Miki Siw was still busy with the fire and did not look up. "I told her. But she wanted to hear you speak. She was alone there."

Moon stared in the direction of York Factory. "At first, I was not so afraid. I wanted her to think I did not come because I knew she would work hard and well. If I went she might think I saw her still as a child needing help. And then, as time passed…it got more difficult. And then I grew too afraid."

Moon looked into the basket, but it was obvious she was not seeing the roots inside. "My thinking was not clear. I did not help my daughter – or myself."

I hesitated. "Perhaps you helped her at the beginning. But she has been there a long time. She has begun to doubt herself." I took Moon's basket from her. "But you will see her in a few weeks. You can tell her then. It would explain a great deal."

Moon looked down at her empty hands. "I will do that."

We were silent for the rest of the afternoon and into the evening. We listened to the snapping and croaking and singing that filled the air, and turned in early. That night I awoke twice. Each time I could make out Moon's silhouette as she sat poking the fire. Before dawn we were all up and quickly ready for the journey. Moon's face was tired and drawn, and though she smiled at me, she said nothing.

Once we were walking, and the chill of the early morning was worn away, I resolved to speak to Miki Siw, hoping to find a way to ease my words without causing Moon further regret. As usual, he was ahead of me. I hurried past Kino and caught up with him. We walked in silence for a time, partly because I was out of breath, and partly so I could compose my words to him. To my surprise, he raised the subject first.

"My thanks for asking my mother about my sister. She did not speak to me. But she speaks clearly to you so that you will understand. I have learned that my sister and I did not understand her ways this time."

"I have upset her."

Miki Siw slowed his pace so that I could keep up.

"She likes us to be strong. But I did not know how to tell her about my sister without making my sister sound weak."

"But we all know she is not!"

Miki Siw continued to stride along, not looking at me. "My mother is used to facing fear. She will go anywhere, say what needs to be said or do what needs doing. She is respected everywhere, as you have seen. I do not say she does not feel fear. But she acts with her fear in her hand. But I did not know why she would not see my sister. I too began to think my mother did not like the work my sister has done there."

I nodded. I was struggling to keep up and had no breath to spare.

"My sister is proud. She needed our mother, but she did not want to ask for fear of disappointing her. When our mother did not choose to see her, we began to wonder at her reasons. We never thought it might be this."

I noticed Kino beside us suddenly. He looked solemn. For a change, he did not scowl at me when I caught his eye. We were in a valley, and the trees that had closed in on us, blocking the sun and crowding us with long brittle branches, had thinned. The grasslands that Miki Siw and Moon and Amelia had told stories about were beginning. The sky opened up above us like a shimmering shell, spilling light and colour on all that lay below.

Kino looked over my head at Miki Siw as we walked. "Your mother," he began, then stopped. He shook his head. "How could she not see your sister? How can she be afraid? Those savages are not worthy of fear. I don't understand."

"Her choice was hard for us all, even knowing the reason now. But everyone feels fear about something, Kino," Miki Siw reminded him.

"But I have seen her stop wars! I have seen her stand between sworn enemies and cause them to be friends. I hear of her walking into the bad death – healing the sick and tending the dead. The things she has done! We have no time for fear!" Kino abruptly set off running, swiftly and silently ahead. We watched him run until he was out of sight.

PAHKEKINWESKISIN – MOCCASIN

That night we met up with a group of English men. We were back along the river and the going got a bit rough passing through bushes and trees, but we would be stopping soon and it was convenient to be near water. Miki Siw told me of their presence ahead long before I heard their noise. As we drew closer, however, the crackling of muskets, the shouts, the noise of the campsite grew loud. Moon walked with us now. Kino was nowhere to be seen. Miki Siw looked inquiringly at Moon to see whether we should approach directly or bypass them. I did not see Moon's signal, but she said to me, "We will see if they need any help."

Although for the last few yards they were in

plain sight to us, the small group (there were five) jerked about as one man when we came into the firelight. As we walked up to the small fire, I saw that their faces above the bushy beards were covered in sores and pustules. I had thought a beard would protect the skin, and many men had them, but Master George had said they were insect traps. One of the men, over his shock sooner than the others, leapt up and begged us for food. Moon pulled out her pemmican supply. It looked untouched from the fort. But then, Miki Siw or Kino or Moon had gathered food every day as we walked. Still, I knew I had far less left than she. She gave it to the man, who thanked her profusely. He immediately dug in before his partners managed to wrest it away from him. The first one, still chewing, pointed at his feet. He was not wearing moccasins or footwear of any sort.

"Need shoes," he mumbled around his full mouth. He hobbled over to a worn, dirty rucksack set near a log, opened it, and rummaged around. He pulled out a couple of ragged moccasins with the bottoms completely worn away. He brought the filthy things over to me and pressed them in my hands. "Need shoes," he said slowly and loudly. He peered into my face, about to say it again, I suspect, when he almost choked on his pemmican. "A little part-white lass! English? Know any English? Français?" he shouted into my face.

His friends, who had begun scrounging around for their own shoe remnants hustled over at his words. Pressing their own bits on top of their mate's, they pushed each other aside to get a look at me. As each one reached for me, one grabbing an arm, another my shoulder, and argued amongst themselves, I pulled back and elbowed them away. I hadn't been treated like baggage for some time.

The pairs of moccasins dropped to the ground. Five pairs of eyes stayed fixed on me until Moon spoke up. "Where is your guide?"

The leader glanced at Moon and then back at me. "He left us –"

"No thanks to you –" one of the men muttered.

"He was to get some more supplies and meet us back here two days ago."

"Where are you going?"

"Norway House."

"Another fort," Miki Siw said, as an explanation to me. He turned back to the men and said, "You are off the path then. You need to –"

Miki Siw's words were drowned out when a great argument broke out amongst the men. Obviously they had each wanted to take a different route back to their post. Accusations and blame flew back and forth. Moon and Miki Siw exchanged glances. One of the men dragged a much crumpled and dirty scrap of paper from his clothes and smoothed it out before handing it to Miki Siw. The leader hobbled over, cursing the stony ground while pointing a stubby dirty finger in anticipation of the map. "We are here, all right? We want to go there!" He tapped the paper officiously.

The other pushed his hand away. "No, no. We're here. We have to follow along this part here first."

That remark started them off again.

Miki Siw held up his hand and the men fell silent. "I will take you to the nearest river portage. Then you will be within a few days' walk to the post."

"But our shoes!" the chorus went up and all eyes returned to me.

"Do you have leather for the soles?" Moon asked politely.

"Hell, yes!" And so we stayed and sewed their moccasins for them. Grudgingly on my part, but with seemingly no bitterness on the part of Moon. George had not ordered me around much once I grew familiar with my duties, at least not as these men tried to – and I realized I had become unaccustomed to it. As a child in London, I had needed guidance and relied on those older and wiser to shelter me. Now, as I myself was getting older and I hoped wiser, I no longer desired to be treated as a child or as chattel.

I remembered Moon's comments along the way when we stopped to help others who had not thought or planned carefully – that we could be in a similar quandary if not for the Great Spirit watching over us. It had seemed, as it did now, however, that Moon, Miki Siw, and even Kino, for all his impulsiveness, would never get into the kinds of fixes some people got themselves into. Like these ones, with leather to spare, but no awl or sinew to attach the soles to the moccasins. When we finished with the moccasins, all a uniform utilitarian brown, one of the men brought over a beaded piece, obviously cut from an old pair of moccasins that had worn away, and he'd saved the design.

"Attach this, if you can," he ordered. I looked at Moon, who was looking at the beaded pattern.

She nodded at me but said under her breath, "do it quickly." My fingers were still sore from pressing the awl through the leather, but I rather messily began to attach the beadwork to the top of the moccasin. When it was completed, Moon took it from me and laid it with the others. She signalled Miki Siw and then nodded at me. I got up and followed her, puzzled. I heard Miki Siw say to the men that it was time to leave. They had chewed their way through a ball of pemmican and were now taking long pulls from a keg.

"Now?" one of the men complained. "Wait, where did those women go?"

Miki Siw said something indistinguishable and we heard groans from the men. Then we were surrounded by birdsong and the sounds of the breeze rustling leaves. Moon waited for me to catch up.

"Are we going to wait for Miki Siw and Kino?"

Kino emerged beside me and I suppressed my surprise. "He will catch up. Did they stink!"

I replied, "And did they ever talk loudly."

Kino raised his voice. "Helps-you-un-der-stand-them!" We followed silently along behind Moon. I continued, "I'm glad we left quickly. I thought we might all have to go with them."

Moon glanced at me over her shoulder. "With those curved patterns? I wasn't going to leave you with them a moment longer."

"Why? It was beaded quite attractively, I thought."

Kino sniggered. "We could have left you alone

to sew his moccasin. He seemed to like you. Then you could have sewn the next curve on for him yourself. He seems over-fond of girls – and drink – if that pattern has anything to say about it."

I pondered that for a moment. I caught up to Moon. "Why didn't the others have decorative covers?"

Moon shrugged a shoulder and continued walking. "Perhaps they did at one time, and just never bothered to keep them. Or maybe they have not done anything that warrants warning – or praising – their actions to others."

Kino was right behind me. "Praising. I like that."

"I have seen some." Moon said, undisturbed.

Kino bent over and whispered in my ear. "In her visions, maybe."

"Kino," Moon said immediately.

"Yes, Aunt," Kino said, straightening.

"You lead for a time."

Kino puffed up his chest. "Yes, Aunt."

Soon he was far in front of us. Moon turned to me and sighed. "That boy." But I saw the glint of amusement in her eyes.

OMISIMIW – OLDER SISTER

The day they found us was cool and overcast. It had been raining intermittently since we had set out on foot at dawn. I heard nothing out of the usual, but Miki Siw and Moon had been restless, frequently turning to look back the way we had come. Kino was behind us, out of sight. At breaks their conversation was curt and limited to practical matters. By mid-afternoon, Kino caught up and said only, "Horses."

We stood together, waiting for them to ride up to us. The muffled thumping of the horses' hooves grew close, and finally they were in sight. The man in the lead, upon seeing us, reined his horse in. Two riders behind him slowed and then stopped. I saw two spare horses tied behind the last rider. Moon walked over with an easy grace and greeted the first man in a different tongue. She was smiling, I saw as she passed me, and then we followed her.

The man in the lead rode a white and brown pony with a magnificently plaited mane and tail. Ornate quillwork bags and straps were attached to its back. It stood unnaturally still. The man's face was painted black and red, and he wore a quilled headband around his forehead. He bowed his head to Moon, as did those behind him. Her face, we saw, was now somber as she waited for him to speak. He greeted each of us, though his eyes passed quickly over me. He spoke a few brief words in greeting, automatically translated for me by Miki Siw, that they had been riding hard, and had not expected us to be as far as we had come.

I looked involuntarily at Kino, who had often taunted me with my ignorance and clumsiness, that we went so slowly because of me and my English incompetence. He saw me look. His lips twitched and his eyes flickered, but he kept his gaze on the speaker. The man cleared his throat, and looked behind at the other men as if for reassurance. Then he reached into one of the panniers on the horse's back and pulled out a crumpled leather object. He looked at it with distaste, then unceremoniously threw it, like a challenge, at Moon's and Miki Siw's feet.

It was, I saw, a leather moccasin. The force of the throw had caused it to unroll from its crumpled state, and the intricate beadwork glinted red in contrast to the steel grey sky. The pattern was dramatic, although so severely stained with blood as to have turned the moccasin a dull, blotchy shade of dark brown. I recognized that moccasin. Fear, so long absent, enveloped me. The air felt chill, and all movement, all life, seemed to halt. In the silence, I looked at the tableau, the men frozen on their horses, and then at the four of us, knowing, but not yet aware, dreading I knew not what.

The man on the horse finally spoke. He gestured disdainfully at the moccasin, he pointed vigorously at the men behind him, to the sky, and finally, proudly, he held out his hands, palm up, to Moon. His eyes, though, held no pride. His expression was stark. I heard Amelia's true name spoken. I looked at Moon, who had stiffened, her head still raised to the man's words, but otherwise she did not move. Miki Siw's fists were uncharacteristically clenched and his jaw tight. He had not translated for some moments. I understood nothing. Kino's mouth was open, and his arms dangled uselessly from slumped shoulders. Moon spoke, questioningly. The man sat tall in his saddle but his voice was soft as he replied to Moon.

When he finished speaking, Moon walked closer to the man and patted the horse's neck. She spoke gently to the man, and he held his head stiffly, his mouth thinned. Again time seemed to freeze, as Moon stood by the horse, her hand now still, her eyes closed. Finally, she spoke again, and the man bowed his head. Then he gestured to the men behind, both of whom were so quiet as to seem a mirage. After a final word to Miki Siw and Kino, and again a quick glance at me, the men turned and rode off.

Kino moved first once they had gone, to grind his heel into the moccasin that lay in the wet and decaying leaves. Then he ran off. At the violent movements, Miki Siw looked up, stared vacantly at me, and also moved away. It was Moon, though, who scared me most. She turned to look at me, and her quick grace, her unyielding form, were gone.

"My daughter is badly hurt. The Murderer – Dyer by English name – was beating Siki. My daughter stepped between them, and sent Siki away, out of the Bay. The Murderer, in a drunken rage, beat my daughter instead. He is now dead by our hands. My daughter has been taken away from that place and she may die. She needs a special healer's knowledge to help her." Moon smoothed her hair with a trembling hand, and slowly, like an old woman, shuffled stiffly off into the trees.

I stood for a moment, hardly able to breathe or think. Reluctantly, I recalled how Dyer had taunted Amelia with his attentions to Siki. Amelia had been troubled by Siki's behaviour – this must have been what she was afraid of, that Siki would take up with Dyer. I picked up the moccasin. It had been recently resoled, and the beaded pattern gleamed hauntingly from the surface. A dangerous man. Dead. He would harm no one else. But Amelia lay dying, when in one more month she would have been safe with her family, away from that deadly cold place. Only a few weeks from happiness. And here I was, safe with her own family and with the best healer, far from her.

I walked with the moccasin over to a dead poplar at the river's edge. The rain had begun once more, cold and drear. The tree gave no shelter with its brittle bare branches, but still I sat down on the broken rocks beneath it and leaned back against its trunk. I stared at the green, swiftly flowing water. Miki Siw joined me there.

"Did you hear?" he asked.

I nodded.

"She will go now. On a horse, till they get a canoe. She will go fast. They will have canoes waiting for her after each portage. My sister –" Miki Siw stopped abruptly, then continued. "I will take you to the fort. Kino will go with my mother to my sister and our people."

Kino, from behind us, coughed softly. "Cousin, you must come back too. She is your sister."

Miki Siw shook his head. "No, I cannot. It would not be wise. It must be you two who go."

In the tense silence that followed, I stirred, and asked, tentatively, "What about drawing me a map? Is it that far to Edmonton House? Or is there some other guide? Then all three of you could return at once."

Kino and Miki Siw looked at each other. The possibilities took hold swiftly.

Miki Siw said, "That one behind, on the black pony, Swift Fox? He travels this way often. Perhaps he –" But then Miki Siw shook his head. "But one of us must go. We told George Talk that we would take you. If he ever found out, then there would be grave trouble."

I protested. "None of you would tell him, and I certainly would not. Amelia is my friend. I would not want her to die without her family, merely so you could fulfil an agreement made before...everything changed."

Kino and Miki Siw said nothing, but Miki Siw shook his head. Kino had taken Dyer's moccasin from me. He was carefully shredding it into minuscule pieces and scattering them in the water. We watched the water flow swiftly towards Amelia. Quickly, quickly, it seemed to say. A muskrat swam past with long grass held in its mouth, its tail tracing a line in the water.

Kino said, "Willa is right. She could go with another." He was silent a moment. Then, with an effort, he said, "I could take her there safely."

Miki Siw and I stared at him in surprise.

He said, more strongly, "I could. I could do it."

After a moment Miki Siw said, hope in his eyes, "Do you know the way well enough, do you think?"

Kino puffed out his chest and was about to answer. Then he thought better of it. He let out his breath and looked at me uncertainly. "I think so. And the way home would be easy canoeing. But I could, perhaps I should, ask the Swift Fox to come with us." He turned to me and said with great courtesy, "You would be safe with me, Willa. I would be sure to get you there without trouble."

"I know you would, Kino," I said. We looked at Miki Siw, but he sat with his arms wrapped around his knees, his head down. Kino stared into the river. We heard the wind whisper in wet grass. We were silent, thinking.

After awhile I asked, "Where did those men go? Are they waiting for you?"

Miki Siw answered without lifting his head. "Yes. My mother has gone to gather healing herbs. Perhaps she can save her. Then we will leave." His voice was harsh.

Kino made a violent movement with his knife. "That snake could not contain his poison."

We sat silent until Moon's soft voice addressed us from behind. Her arms were full of plants, and she sat down gracefully and began stripping leaves and placing them in one pile and the stems in another. We each reached for a plant and began to follow her lead. Once she had us started, she started on a different plant, carefully separating the root from the stem, and setting it in a small heap. As we worked, she explained what each plant was for. She pulled some soft white skins from a packsack and carefully slid each separate grouping into a separate bag. As she did so she went over each – its name, its use, its application. Miki Siw repeated each, as did Kino. Although Kino looked mystified, Miki Siw's face was grim.

Moon looked intently at Miki Siw. Her face was full of pain, but her voice was even. "I will take Willa to the fort. I made that promise to my daughter, and I will keep it though she may not live. You and Kino must go swiftly, swiftly. I have asked for –" she said a word in her own language and then turned to me, "– a great healer – to go to my daughter. If she is there, give her these herbs. She will help."

Kino broke the shocked silence that greeted her words. "Why must you go? Willa will tell no one who takes her there. Or if it must be one of us, it could be me. I could take her to the fort." Kino appealed to me. "You can trust me," he said. He continued to look straight at me, without his usual arrogance. In fact, I realized in surprise, he was treating me with the same respect he showed Moon and Miki Siw.

"I know I can," I said again. We all waited for Moon to speak.

Moon waited while we thought about his words. Then she said, "That is an honourable offer, Kino. I know you could take Willa there and come back safely. But it is not that. You say no one would know. But I would know. My daughter would know. I do not want to fail her again."

"How would you fail her, Moon, by going to her now?" I asked. "I don't understand."

Moon rubbed her neck and then, for a moment, put her head on her knees as Miki Siw had done. When she looked up, she said simply, "My daughter asked me to take you safely to the new fort. I agreed. If I do not honour her request, then I fail her. By doing what she asked of me, I show respect. If I return to her now without fulfilling our agreement, then I would be saying that what she thought important was not what I thought important."

"But did Amelia say it had to be you? Was that part of the agreement you made? Would she not understand that you changed the agreement out of your concern for her life?"

"She said I must take you. I want to take you. I want to ensure you are safe. I have to hold faith with my daughter. She would want that."

Kino coughed, and when he spoke his voice was harsh. "Even if she dies? You would leave her there without your care in order to take Willa to a fort that many others could also do? You are her only mother, but there are many other guides."

"Kino, it is not about guiding. It is about honour. If I returned to try to heal my daughter without having fulfilled our agreement, then whether she lives or dies, she and her spirit would not be happy. I must do what she asked. It may be the last thing she is able to ask me to do. And I will do it. I will not disappoint her again."

In the painful quiet, Moon added, "We need to speak more of this, but there is no time. My daughter may die. I do not want that to happen. You must go."

Miki Siw took a bag and carefully slid the plant pieces inside and gently pulled the flap and tied the strings. He didn't look at his mother. "We will be swift. Willa will go quickly as well. Perhaps you could take her to Kewitin, and Kewitin could take her the last two days. You could take Kewitin's canoe...."

Moon shook her head. "I will take Willa to the fort. That is what I will do. And when that is done I will return to our homeplace. Only then." Her hands were steady but her voice, though firm, was like dust. The bones of her face shadowed her eyes.

We worked quickly. Then Moon stood up and said, "I will tell the men you are ready."

The three of us scrambled up and watched her

go. Kino grabbed the discarded stalks and threw them hard in the river. We watched as some swirled and caught in the grasses by the shore. Others sailed quickly out of sight, while still others got caught in a current and went under.

Miki Siw moved to his leather bag and pulled out his pemmican. He parted the meat in two, and pressed the larger half into my hands. "Make sure that she eats. Give her what pemmican is left after you get to the fort. We thought we'd have time to spend with some people there, but my mother must come back. The less reason she has to delay her return, the sooner she will be with us."

Kino pulled out his roll of fur he used now the nights had turned colder. He looked at me with a wry expression. "Take this, Willa. There will not be time to build shelters. And you are always cold at night."

I took it from him slowly. "My thanks."

"Safe journey, my friend," Kino replied.

"Is there anything else I can do?" I asked.

Miki Siw rubbed his forehead. "Just travel long days. Rise early. And hope that my mother returns before my sister goes to the Great Mother. My sister would want to see her mother before she dies."

"*If* she dies. She may yet live. We must hope."

Kino repeated, "She may live. She is strong."

I looked from him to Miki Siw. "Will your father know?"

Miki Siw shook his head. "He will be too far into the sacred place. We can't hope to reach him in time. Unless he sees her in a vision and returns early. Otherwise he has never yet returned before the homecoming."

"How hurt is she? Was she able to tell them what had happened?"

Miki Siw frowned. "Oh yes, I did not translate that. They cannot awaken her. She is in a deep sleep. Her head is hurt. Her body was –" Miki Siw looked away and did not speak.

Kino continued, "Others told the tale. Talk Too Much dragged Dyer away from my cousin. He called our people and fought Dyer until they came. He said the man would be reprimanded. Reprimanded!" He and Miki Siw exchanged angry looks.

"And Siki?"

"She is back with her people. She will have his child."

Kino ground his teeth. "Me, I am glad he is dead and his bones ground to dust and his head on a stick. I hope he suffered long."

"Master George did that?"

Kino looked at me with surprise. "No. Others

did. Talk Too Much was badly wounded. Dyer stabbed him." He paused for a moment, thinking. "But, you know, he did not even speak when others dealt with Dyer. Nor did any other of the Company men interfere. Is that not rare, Cousin?"

Miki Siw was not really listening to us. He blinked. "What? Oh. George can be a good man at times. He had learned of Amelia's gifts. He knew Dyer breathed venom."

The men on the horses rode back to the clearing and Moon greeted them. She turned to Miki Siw and they spoke privately. Then Miki Siw and Kino quickly jumped to the backs of the two spare horses. Without any ceremony the five horses and their riders wheeled round and galloped off.

Moon stood watching for a few moments after they had gone. Then she turned to me. "There is nothing keeping us here. Shall we go as well?"

I agreed, and went to get my pack.

MISIWÂPOS, *TIPISKÂW PÎSIM* – HARE AND MOON

I had expected Moon to quicken our pace, and was prepared to walk in my sleep if necessary, but she kept to the same even stride that we had always used once I had become accustomed to walking all day. She ate little, however, and would only occasionally take a drink of water, and only then when I offered it, never of her own volition. She walked steadily and silently, her mind turned inward. I kept up and kept silent.

Moon and I travelled for ten more days. The next would be my last with her, she said. We stopped early that afternoon. After gathering deadfall, she sat for a long time before the unlighted fire. Quietly, and very slowly, she unplaited her hair. This, I knew from Amelia, was a sign of mourning. I brought water from the river, stones for the fire, more deadfall for the night, and gathered tea leaves for our tea, and still she did not move. Finally, I walked over and sat down beside her.

"You can go to her, Moon," I said.

Moon laid a twig gently on the stack of wood. In a low voice she said, "My daughter grows weaker. I can hardly feel her spirit." She looked at her empty hands, hands that were never still, until now. "I must go to her," she said.

I put my hand on top of hers. "You must," I said.

Moon drew a deep breath. "I grow old. My strength is not great. I have not travelled so far for many moons. But I must try. I don't want to leave you alone here, but where I go is very dangerous. You would be safer to stay here. You may choose."

I nodded, bewildered. "I will come with you," I said.

Moon's hand tightened on mine. "We have no one to watch over us. We must light a large fire to keep animals away while we are gone. You must take care, Willa."

"I will do what you say," I said.

Moon bent her head once more, her loosened

hair obscuring her face. "Then I must plan," she said softly.

She said nothing else to me. As early afternoon faded into late afternoon, I gathered more and more deadfall until the pile towered above my head. The river, teeming with fish, offered up two large ones for our meal, and hesitantly I cleaned them, wrapped them, started a small fire, and steamed them. I was relieved when Moon came out of her reverie, but she refused to eat or drink. I drank tea, and then we prepared ourselves for the night.

I wrapped myself in Kino's fur and then in my blanket. I watched Moon as she rebuilt the fire. She hauled large logs into a criss-crossed square and then built a square house of logs on top. She took our fire-poking stick and manoeuvred the burning logs in a ring around the wooden tower, leaving a gap between them and the centre. She added kindling all around the circle, and soon it burned brightly. When it reached its peak burn, I realized, its heat and flame would catch the tower on the inside and burn intensely and long, while the outer ring would slowly die out. It was not yet cold, but I could feel a chill creeping in. Moon did not wrap herself up. She did not lie down. She came to where I lay and sat down, cross-legged, beside me. She bent her head, and began, ever so softly, to chant. It went on, quietly, evenly. I slept uneasily, then I woke, then slept again. Still Moon chanted. Eventually the moon rose, white and round above the dark emerald treetops. The sky was black and clear and full of stars. The air was very cold and still. I glanced at Moon, whose eyes were now shut, her breathing even. She looked peaceful; the lines on her face smoothed. Her beautiful black hair showed threads of silver I had not noticed before.

I pulled Kino's fur more tightly around my neck. My movement startled something; I heard a snapping sound in the trees. I felt my heart stop. Moon suddenly looked up and, without pausing, stood in one fluid motion. She began to walk away from the fire without looking back. I sat up. Where was she going? At any other time I would not have been overly concerned, though it was rare for us to leave the fire once we'd retired for the night. But after our conversation this afternoon, I was not so sure. I rose slowly, straining my eyes to see where she had gone. I edged around the fire, keeping my eyes away from its brightness. The moon lit a path, and I saw Moon walking within its silvery band of light. She was going away. I swallowed hard, then I followed. Moon turned when she heard me behind her and held a finger to her lips. She pointed at the moonlit path and shook a finger at the blackness beyond. Do not go off the path, I knew she meant. I would not. We walked in darkness. The wind picked up and blew. Dust swirled around us and still we walked. I could not feel my legs after a time. I dropped my blanket somewhere, and when I turned to pick it up, it was gone. Animals howled and drew near us as we journeyed. Once I saw a large black bear keeping pace with Moon, and overhead, out of sight, an eagle keened. Moon ignored them, and I, with a quick prayer, tried to do the same. We walked in trees, through bog, over rock. The steely cold turned to snow and then sleet and then, finally, to warmth. We walked on a carpet of red leaves and gold, the wind died, a cloud slid quietly across the moon. And we were there.

)) ● ((

I heard the chanting first. Then the beat of a drum. Slowly, slowly. As we walked along the path, the chanting grew louder. First I saw a very young child holding a feather. She handed the feather to Moon, then she turned and seemed to whisper to another. As Moon took the feather, the chanting grew louder and I watched people line the pathway, eerily silent, quietly solemn. They were not the chanters, though the sound grew louder. They all faced in the direction we walked, and they said nothing.

We walked until we reached a conical tipi, and another small child held open the flap. As Moon bent to enter, I hesitated to follow, but the small child smiled at me and beckoned me inwards. I went within. There, I was overwhelmed by beauty. The walls of the tipi were covered with an interior liner that was painted and quilled and woven. The beauty of life was on those walls, and I felt the strength of spirit clear the darkness from around us. My eyes were full of these wonders as I turned to the centre, where an ornately embroidered blanket covered a small mound. Beside it knelt a man. Miki Siw, Kino, and an older woman were next to him. The older woman had a cloth in her hands and a container with a sweet-smelling herb inside. They looked at us as we entered, and their eyes were filled with unutterable sadness. The man half-rose to greet Moon, but put his hand on his throat, as if to say he could not speak. I joined Kino beside the blanket and sat cross-legged. With a shock, I realized the blanket covered Amelia. Such a small mound.

Moon knelt and gently turned down the blanket. The man carefully lifted Amelia up so Moon could hold her in her arms, but Amelia's eyes did not open. She wore only a leather shift. Her arms, exposed, were skeletal. Her breathing was faint, and in fact I hardly knew if she lived. It was painful to look at her, but Moon did not flinch. She began to speak the story of Amelia's life. At first I could not understand, since she spoke in their language. And then, somehow, I could. She held Amelia, all the while, in her arms. She spoke to Amelia as if she were awake and could hear. And, ah, the stories she told. As she told about Amelia's brave exploits, her brilliance as an interpreter, her many achievements in her life, we all listened. When she began to tell of the mischievous things Amelia had done as a girl – and oh there were many! – the man, Amelia's father, began to laugh as he remembered, and the tears ran down his face. I felt the cold in my spine dissolve, and Kino, then Miki Siw, also laughed, and embellished the stories. We heard about the tiny bear cub Amelia brought home, to her parents' shock, the trap she built to capture a disliked playmate, the first hated moccasins she quilled.... Moon talked on and on, without a break, pausing only to sip a drink that the older woman would provide. After a long time, the father also moved close, putting one arm around Moon and the other on Amelia. He added his voice to Moon's and between them they spoke, they sang, they chanted. Moon told her daughter how proud she was of all Amelia had done, how bleak life was while she was away, and how much more Amelia had to do, and would do, together with her family. Always together, Moon repeated. Amelia's work was not yet done.

And then, an eternity later, Amelia's eyes opened. Moon quickly put a drink to her lips. Amelia weakly raised a hand and placed it on Moon's cheek. All was still. Then all leaned forward as one, and Amelia touched each of them. Then she saw me, and she smiled, and slowly she reached out her hand. Carefully, I took it. Though I could feel the bones in her fingers, her hand seemed to grow warmer even as I held it. Amelia then let go of my hand and turned back to her mother. The heat of an invisible fire reached me, and I blinked in surprise. And then I could not see.

I felt the fall of darkness around me. I opened my eyes and found myself standing near the fire Moon and I had built. The centre burned furiously, the outer circle now ash. The moon was low in the sky, but brilliant rays still stemmed outward. It was very cold; frost glistened everywhere. In a tree on the other side of the fire, I saw an enormous golden eagle perched on a branch, watching us. I saw Moon sitting cross-legged by the fire, her face partly visible in moonlight. I picked up Kino's fur and wrapped it around me from where it had fallen from my shoulders. I heard a sharp snap and I whirled. Reflected in the moon and firelight was the largest hare I had ever seen. Its fur had already turned white; the tips shone silver in the moonlight. Only one haunch had a tinge of brown, hinting of the warm summer past. I stood still and watched it watch me with its great black eyes. Cautiously, it turned its head to look at Moon, and then limped slowly, trembling, through the frozen grass to where she sat. It gazed long into her face. It moved awkwardly, as if it had been hurt and was not yet entirely healed.

A thin shadow slid across the brilliance of the moon and dimmed its rays before gleaming forth once more. A breeze began to blow, swirling ashes from our fire, and I shivered involuntarily. The hare turned its dark, unfathomable eyes back to me as if concerned. Frost clung to its nose and whiskers and I could see its breath. Moon reached out her fingers to the hare and whispered weakly, "I am fine. Go back, please, and heal." In the ghostly silence the hare leaped high over Moon's form. I watched it bound away, gone instantly, disappearing into the night without a sound. I looked at Moon, who smiled past me and said, "You as well." In the blackness past the fire, I saw a darker, bearlike shape back away from us. The golden eagle took flight. I went over to her then and wrapped Kino's fur around her shoulders. We sat still and silent until morning.

AMISKWACIWÂSKAHIKAN – EDMONTON HOUSE

At sunrise, I looked for signs of the hare. All I found were maple leaves of red and gold, blown far from their home by the wind in the night. But Moon washed the soot and the sorrow from her face. She neatly replaited her black and silver hair, saying simply, in response to my unasked question, "She lives."

We expected to reach the new fort by midday: Edmonton House. Moon said that it stood above the river on a steep bank.

"You don't need to take me right to the fort," I said to Moon. "I can find it from here. You go."

Moon was very tired, and very weak. She did

not look well. But she smiled and said, "I will see you to the fort."

I led the way at times, and she seemed pleased at the decisions I made. She questioned me on uses of some of the plants and shrubs near the river and seemed satisfied with my answers. The vegetation rose high and abundant above the river, so different from York Factory on Hudson's Bay. The leaves were already turning and falling, and we trod on hues of orange and yellow.

Moon said, "I hope you like your new home. The winters are cold and long, but not like where you were. And here there are many warm days." She paused. "There is a man here called Thomas Web. He will be a friend. Tell him you know my family, and if you ever have need, he will be able to call us."

We were very near the fort now. There were many tipis set up below the hill in front of the fort. The people there had seen us. One at once lifted a canoe over her head and began to carry it towards the river. Carved and painted, and sealed, it was beautiful. Others carried bundles. They hastened towards us. They had heard word, then, about Moon and Amelia.

I could see the fort gates and two men standing talking at the entrance. I stopped and turned to

Moon, to thank her for bringing me here safely, and for all she had done for me along the way.

Moon took my hands. "We will see each other again, Willa."

We watched as one of the men started walking towards us. Moon released my hands and I blinked back tears. Again I was in a new place surrounded by strangers. How would I manage here?

"We will see each other again, soon," Moon repeated. She took the pemmican I held out, and then she turned and walked towards the women.

I greeted the man and told him my name, and I watched as Moon disappeared into the willows. It was hard not to follow. Soon, she had said. I recall her words clearly.

But it has been long.

AFTERWORD

In *Willa's New World* the characters are fictional. There was a man named George in charge of York Factory then, but the similarity ends there. On the other hand, in this story many of the events and circumstances surrounding the characters are true. For instance, York Factory really was a Hudson's Bay Company trading post first built in 1684. The climate, animals, and vegetation are all drawn from books I have read. The kinds of life and events described did occur – the cold, dark winters, the long trips via rivers and land, the relationships between First Peoples and Europeans – were typical. The supply ships arrived and left at the approximate times stated in the book. York Factory began building York boats and trading posts inland in order to compete with others who were making inroads on the Hudson's Bay Company profits. Edmonton House (or Fort Edmonton) was built in 1795.

There were Home Guard Cree who lived and worked in and around York Factory. They and other First Peoples groups acted as liaisons between and among different bands. They also taught the Europeans survival techniques and geography, and provided most of the food, wood, clothing, and other necessities of life to those who lived at York Factory. They were, therefore, responsible for the many duties I have mentioned.

Of course, First Peoples were an integral part of the fur trade everywhere, not just at York Factory or with the Hudson's Bay Company. Without their knowledge, Europeans could neither have survived nor been able to profit from furs. Trading of goods and information among First Peoples was common and extensive.

One perhaps lesser known fact is the important role First Peoples women played not only in the fur trade but also in their own societies. Women were seen as physically very strong. They had great endurance, and carried most of the heavy loads. They were able to travel long distances, often with little food to sustain them. The women gathered and prepared the food, made the clothing, bore and looked after the children, and served as guides, hard labourers, and interpreters on journeys. There are stories about women who were outstanding interpreters, guides, and diplomats in addition to their many other responsibilities. Therefore, while Amelia's family and their work as healers, guides, information couriers, and traders are fictional, their skills are drawn from what I have read.

I based Willa, Moon, Miki Siw, and Kino's journey on the approximately four months it took to travel from York Factory to Edmonton House. It is about 1500 kilometres from York Factory to Edmonton House as the crow flies, but depending on the exact route travellers might take, it could be as long as 2000 to 2500 kilometres. When travelling on foot, this means walking about 15 to 20 kilometres per day.

Of course, some of the details are made up, such as moccasins carrying meanings about the wearers, or that various bands had "spies" in their midst, although both are possible. I deliberately did not specify where Amelia, Moon, Miki Siw and Kino Sesis came from, or which band they were part of. There is a possibility that they could be Cree, but not Swampy Cree, some of whom were part of the Home Guard.

First Peoples experienced horrible deaths from smallpox and other European diseases to which they had no resistance. Many history books describe the anguish with which some of them died from smallpox. Many other diseases, such as typhus, scarlet fever, measles, and influenza, also raged through their communities.

The plants Amelia, Moon, Miki Siw, Kino, and others collected and used are based on references to plants used by Natives historically (purple coneflower, for instance, that Amelia recommends for Digger's leg, is Echinacea, a widely known native plant that is effective for use on wounds, cuts, gangrene, infection, and so on).

Staffing was a perennial problem for all of the Hudson's Bay Company forts. Even so, European women and children were not officially allowed to travel to any of the forts without the knowledge and approval of the London Committee during the time period that I write.

That is why I have Willa's great-uncle bribe a ship's captain to take her to Hudson Bay. Supply ship captains had a great deal of power in those days, but acting against the London Committee's orders would have been risky. Even today, however, men, women, and children are smuggled illegally into different countries by various means, and if they're not caught, then few are the wiser.

Acknowledgements

Working on a project like this requires a great deal of research as well as advice and information from many people. I was very fortunate to be able to prevail upon two stellar historians in Edmonton to read my manuscript and make comments. Dr. Ian MacLaren gave me excellent editorial advice and corrections on this manuscript and directed me to sources where I could find further information. Dr. Michael Payne's fascinating book entitled *The Most Respectable Place in the Territory: Everyday Life in Hudson's Bay Company Services York Factory, 1788 to 1870* and his dissertation, "Daily Life on Western Hudson Bay 1714 to 1870: A Social History of York Factory and Churchill," are two sources that contain a wealth of information on this time period. Michael also took time to help me fit fiction with fact, and was gracious and understanding when fiction sometimes took precedence over historical reality.

Arlene Kissau, Acting Director at the St. Albert Public Library and Doug Cuthand, a journalist and film and television producer in Saskatoon, both read the manuscript from different perspectives and gave me valuable feedback that I was able to incorporate into the manuscript.

I referred to dictionaries for Cree words and translations. In particular, the *Alberta Elders' Cree Dictionary alperta ohci kehtehayak nehiyaw otwestamâkewasinahikan* by Nancy LeClair and George Cardinal was a great final resource.

While I researched many books, journals, and archival records over the years, two books on women in the fur trade were especially valuable: *"Many Tender Ties": Women in Fur-Trade Society in Western Canada, 1670-1870* by Sylvia Van Kirk and *Strangers in Blood: Fur Trade Company Families in Indian Country*, by Jennifer S.H. Brown.

The poem I have Master George quote from is an excerpt from a work by another George, Lord

Byron (1788-1824), who wrote the poem called "Darkness."

My family helped me with this project over the years as I picked it up and set it down. Without my sister Debra Demers-Bryan's frequent reminders to work on the manuscript, it would have remained incomplete much longer! I did have an incentive to finish, however, Debra agreed to provide the fine illustrations that now grace the interior. My mother, Verna Demers, read the manuscript numerous times with an eye for what younger readers might like to read. My husband, Steven Williams, provided advice and many reference books that I used to construct the landscape for Willa's experience at Hudson Bay and her journey west. My daughter, Tessia, read the manuscript twice for me – the first time when she was only eight. Her enthusiasm and perceptive suggestions helped me immeasurably.

Lastly, I would like to thank my editor at Coteau Books, Barbara Sapergia, for her thoughtful, thorough, and sensitive editing of *Willa's New World.* As a writer herself, Barbara has given me insights into the writing process that will serve me well in future. Thanks also to Geoffrey Ursell, Nik Burton, Duncan Campbell, Karen Steadman, and other Coteau staff for their support and professional dedication throughout. It has been a pleasure and a privilege to work with Coteau Books.

Barbara Demers

ABOUT THE AUTHOR

BARBARA DEMERS works as an editor in St. Albert, Alberta. She has a BA from the University of Saskatchewan and is pursuing a Master of Education degree. Barbara currently works for the Athabasca University.

Born in Edmonton, she lived in Australia and New Zealand for a time before returning to Alberta to work. *Willa's New World* is her first book.